# REINING IN THE REBEL

## TALL, DARK & DRIVEN ~ BOOK THREE

### BARBARA DELEO

# REINING IN THE REBEL

*Tall, Dark and Driven—Book 3*
***Ari's story***
by Barbara DeLeo

*This book was previously published, in part, as Four Weddings and a Fling*

*D*amn!

Ari Katsalos carefully lifted the motorcycle helmet he'd thrown onto wedding planner Grace Bennett's desk and let out another curse.

Some kind of pastel headband thing with flowers sticking up was now a mash of fabric and bits of wire. Stark white ribbon leaned at a drunken angle, and sparkly bits had broken off and fallen on the floor. Considering how surprised—and probably pissed—Grace was going to be when she found him sitting behind her desk in his parents' wedding hall, this wasn't a great start.

As he looked around, the muscles across his shoulders tensed. This might be his family's comfort zone, and no doubt Grace's, but it gave him a bad case of wanna-get-the-hell-out.

Marriage and weddings. Did anyone actually believe in those things anymore? Definitely not the cheating spouses he made his living out of. He was booked solid for the next few months, which made having to juggle his PI business with this place a nightmare. But sometimes family and duty called, so here he was, drowning in fluff and fantasies.

Retrieving the mangled decoration, he carefully covered it with a bit of pink lacy fabric and decided to tell Grace about it when the time was better.

She'd be making her way across the courtyard from the Palace's kitchens about now. He'd left a message saying she was needed urgently in her office, and so she'd be walking through that door in three...two...one...

"Ari, what are you doing here?"

Grace stood at the open door, her delicate fingers gripping the edge, a blush tinting her pale cheeks. "I wasn't expecting you. I thought your sister would be taking over again. Or maybe even your parents...?"

He pushed the chair back and stood, his gaze trained on her arched neck, her milky skin, and the tiny frown crumpling her forehead. It had been a while since he'd seen Grace Bennett, but each time they'd met, a zap of electricity shot through the room.

*Just like one did now.*

He swallowed hard. The way she was desperately trying to focus on anything but him said she felt it too.

So, if they had such great chemistry, why hadn't she wanted to go beyond their one and only date?

With her sexy presence and confident smile, Grace was the type of girl guys dreamed of settling down with. Yeah, maybe that was it—since he wasn't into long-term commitments, it was probably for the best. Didn't account for why he hadn't been able to get her out of his head for the last few months though. And now he was going to do more than think about her. Over the next few weeks, they'd spend a lot more time together than either of them had expected. Only she didn't know that yet.

He slung a hand in his pocket and got straight to the

point. "Yasmin and her fiancé are staying a bit longer in Greece than they'd first planned—catching up with my parents for the next month. Have a seat." He gestured for her to sit at her desk.

She stayed motionless, the floor space a barrier between them as she slowly smiled. "I didn't think you'd be interested in looking after the Palace for your parents like your brother and sister did." She tilted her head playfully. "I can't imagine you buried in wedding lace and garter belts."

*Zap. The power jolt again.*

He grinned. She didn't seem as put out as he'd expected. "Being the only Katsalos left in Brentwood Bay and having this responsibility isn't my idea of fun, believe me." He waved his arm toward her chair again. "Sounds like you've got everything pretty much under control anyway."

She held his gaze as she moved past a mannequin dressed in a ton of white fabric. Her dark copper hair swung just beneath her jawbone, the soft fabric of her flowery dress whispering against her legs.

"So," she said, picking up his helmet and handing it to him. She lifted the lacy pink fabric and a brief cloud crossed her face when she noticed the twisted crown thing, but she carried on. "The first thing you'll need to know is that I'll be leaving next Monday. We've got two big weddings this weekend, but then there's nothing major booked for the next two weeks, so you should be okay. I'm really sorry the timing's so bad. I know some great temp planners who could step in 'til your family gets back." She cleared her throat. "Of course I'll try to help your parents out any way I can."

He took the helmet and put it on a chair. "Leaving?" The breath he let out was sharper than he'd intended. "Because it's me who's in charge? Why don't I know about this?" Tension rolled up his spine one vertebra at a time. How in hell could he run this place on his own?

The last time they'd seen each other, when his brother, Nick, was looking after the Palace, it was only for a few minutes. The time before that had been much more memorable. They'd been on her doorstep, after that first—and last—date, when he'd leaned in for a kiss. She'd gotten all flustered and stepped inside so fast he was left standing like a cartoon cat with its head spinning. He'd called her the next day, but she'd said she was busy, and…he could take a hint. Seemed Grace Bennett thought she was a cut above a tattooed PI from the city.

She smiled, and it blew away some of the tension in the room. "No, it's not you. It's something I've been planning for a long time, but as you know, things have been extra busy here in the last few months, and with all your mom and dad's problems, I didn't want to throw that into the mix. I'd thought Yasmin and Lane would come back after their trip to Italy, so now seemed a good time to step aside. I'm really sorry, but I've made plans."

He rested his hands low on his hips. "You figure the best time to leave the sinking ship is when my parents are on the other side of the world trying to save their marriage? You'd walk out and leave everything to a guy who knows nothing about weddings and who doesn't have anything close to your skill set? Yasmin said you did a great job together when she was redecorating the place, and Nick said the same when he was making the structural changes. Did you plan on leaving when they were in charge?"

This could not be happening. His parents' marriage was on the brink of divorce, and the last thing he wanted to do was destroy their business. He had to fix this.

She took a step back, her lips pressed together.

Of course. She didn't want to work with him. He'd bet his bike that, up until thirty seconds ago, Grace Bennett was happy enough to support his family in this business, and now she wanted out. And that was going to cause a megastorm of problems, not the least of which would be that he'd be here on his own, actually in charge of brides and weddings. He shuddered and rubbed a hand across the back of his neck. "When did you decide to go? Dad never mentioned you leaving."

She lifted her gaze. "Ari, no one's more sorry than I am that your mom and dad are going through a rough time. In the last three years, Mano and Pia have become like family to me, but it's time I moved on. I've found a great site for my own store, and I'll open within a couple of months. From what your mom said the last time we spoke, she wasn't even sure she was coming back to the States, let alone Brentwood Bay."

She already had a plan for what to do when she left? He scrubbed a hand across his chin. "Leaving's not an option." He shook his head, his stomach clenching. "You're the only person who can help me here. I need you, Grace."

A flush swept up her neck as she rearranged the pile of fabric on her desk.

"And if that's not enough, my entire family needs you too."

She nibbled at her bottom lip and shook her head. "I'd love to help you out, but the timing's just all wrong. I'm really sorry, Ari."

He pulled up a chair, turned it backward and straddled it. "I might've grown up in this business, but I've been a PI for the past six years." He held her gaze to let her know how serious he was. "Want to know how much I know about wedding dresses and bridezillas these days?" He dragged a finger through the air across his throat. "Nada." He dropped his voice. "Want to know how much I *intend* learning about wedding dresses and bridezillas? Double nada. But no decent person would stand by and watch all his parents' hard work over the last thirty years go down the john. If you leave now, the Aegean Palace is finished. And I'd bet my bike that you don't want to see that happen."

She hesitated and emotion blossomed on her face. "I'm sure I could find a temp for you by the time I leave." She pulled her cell toward her. "Let me give a couple of them a call."

"I don't want anyone else."

He drew in a slow, calming breath and waited until she'd swung her gaze to his again and the air sparked. "I want you." He crossed his arms on the back of the chair. "Grace, you understand this place. You're the only reason it's survived all the craziness, and only you can keep things running smoothly. I can't call in a temp PI. I've gotta keep my own business going, so if you're not here, we'll all be screwed." He tried a grin. "I'll beg if it helps."

She pushed a shining strand of hair back from her face and tucked it behind her ear. "I'm sorry, Ari. I'd really like to help, but I can't. You'll find a replacement for me in no time."

He rolled his shoulders. If they lost her, then the whole business would crumble, and there'd be nothing for his father to bring his mother back to. And, above everything, he wanted his parents home and back together.

"I understand you're feeling unsettled without my mom and dad here, but couldn't you wait until they get back to open your store? Everyone knows you've been the best thing to happen to this business in years."

*And I want to see that for myself.*

"I've put a deposit on a store lease, and I can't afford to pay rent without it earning for me." She tapped her fingers on her chin, the other hand still resting on her phone. Was that hesitation in her voice? "My best friends, Lettie and Meg, are coming to work for me, and I can't let them down. I was hoping to start work as soon as possible."

He held her gaze. "What sort of store?"

"Wedding accessories with a planning service." She rolled her fingers across a line of sharpened colored pencils on the desk. "I need to spread my wings, and now's the best time to do it." For the first time since she'd come into the room, her face was lit, her movements animated.

He rested his chin on his fist and surveyed her. "Maybe, but there's no time to get someone used to the way things are done around here. You said yourself there are weddings this weekend. What if I thought of a way to help you kick off your new business while you're still working here?"

She leveled him with her stunning blue-eyed stare. "Like what?"

Now was not the time to get completely and utterly lost in those eyes, but another time, another place…

He stood and held his hands out, palms up, his mind tripping over itself in the rush to come up with a solution. "What if you set up your business but make a commitment to work on contract with us for the rest of this season, just until things are back to normal? It'd mean you keep an income while you incur all your setup costs, and we get a transition back to my family running things. We can put your name and all your new business information on any of our advertising from now on."

She paused, her head tilted on the slightest of angles. "So, I'd only need to be here for the next month or so, and during that time you'd let me set up my own business and promote myself as an independent service?"

It sounded even better when she said it.

"Yeah, just until one of my family steps back in. But I'd want you to manage the bookings the same way you normally would. You'd be here when you were needed, which could be quite a bit since I've got a whole lot of work for my own business." He pulled a wallet from his jeans pocket, opened it, and handed her a card. "You can call me anytime. I keep some pretty strange hours, but if you ever need me, I'll be here." He nodded at the broken crown on her desk and grinned. "And I'll try not to screw things up."

She put the card on the corner of her desk and sat back in the chair, her shoulders relaxing. "And you wouldn't mind if I was working with my own clients while I'm running things here?"

"Why should I? We'd keep you on as a contractor, so you could recommend the Palace as a venue sometimes, and we could all benefit. And maybe your friends could be getting things set up for you in the meantime."

She slowly nodded, and her face brightened. "Just a month or so? And then you'd take things over?"

Ari laughed. She clearly wasn't a very good judge of character. If he took over the Palace alone, there'd be a helluva lot more broken than a few wedding crowns. If that happened, there wouldn't be any sort of business here by the time his parents got back. "Hell, no. I'm never going to take things over, and no one in my family would let me. I'm just keeping an eye on things, then I'm out of here. I've rented an office in town. But, as I said, call me anytime."

She tapped her fingers on the desk. "It would be good to still base myself here for a couple of weeks until my place is ready. And we are busy this weekend… You know I've been living in the apartment out back? Could I stay there for now?"

"Of course."

He made a mental note to respect her privacy, but it was a good feeling—thinking of her being here full time.

She rolled her lips together. "I've been so focused on the store I haven't gotten around to organizing a new apartment."

"That's settled then," Ari said, trying to hide a sigh of

relief. "I'll call Dad tonight and let him know what you've decided. From now on, you're Grace Bennett, independent wedding planner, and you're going to make sure I don't mess this place up."

Early the next afternoon, Grace signed her name to the bottom of a flower order and sat back in her chair. Normally at this time of day, she'd be in Pia Katsalos's kitchen eating Greek honey cookies and talking about fantasy weddings. She missed her real boss, and now she had her third one in the last few months—Pia's son, Ari, who wore raw masculinity like a well-cut suit. And if only he *did* wear a suit, instead of the black T-shirt that so perfectly defined his chest and the faded jeans that hugged his strong thighs, maybe then she could concentrate on her work.

When Pia Katsalos had spoken of her youngest son, there had often been sadness in her voice—as if she didn't really know him anymore. According to Pia, Ari hadn't been the star athlete that Nick had been, or the brilliant academic type, like his sister Yasmin. No, when Pia spoke about Ari, it was of a boy who took risks and ran with a different sort of crowd. Someone who was a mystery, especially to those closest to him.

By finishing work in her office, avoiding him today hadn't been hard, but now she needed to confirm some things with Pavlo, the new chef, and she'd seen Ari walking into the restaurant. She was becoming increasingly unsure about working for him. He didn't understand a thing about running a wedding hall and seemed to be the type who had pretty strong opinions on things.

And then there were those muscles and that sexy way his mouth moved when he grinned…

Her phone rang—Lettie, one of her best friends.

"Chick," Lettie said, before Grace had even said hello. "Please tell me you've spent all day staring at that Greek god."

Grace groaned and pressed the heel of her palm to her forehead. "Argh! What am I gonna do, Let? He said he was going to be working from his office in town, but he seems to come and go whenever he feels like it. Maybe I should just tell him that I'll be fine on my own for now and he should go back to the city. That way I won't have to be around him."

*Or stare at that mouth and wonder what it would feel like having those lips pressed against my skin.*

"Hot looks, great bod…why not have those in your face twenty-four-seven?" Lettie asked, a laugh in her voice. "I would. And it'll do you good."

"I dunno," she said. "It's like those cop shows."

"The ones you watched back-to-back when you were going through your divorce?" Her friend's voice was softer.

Back then she'd been trying to convince herself there were still some good men in the world. Men who wanted to protect their women, men who believed in love and honor, not suspicion and control. The second she'd said, "I do," her husband, Mark, had changed from sexy and playful to unpredictable and intense. Slowly, she'd begun to second-guess herself—never able to please him—and by the end of their marriage she'd wondered how she could've ever fallen in love with someone like him.

"You know something?" she said to Lettie. "Ari looks exactly like the cops on those shows."

Dark eyes verging on black, framed by even darker brows, with pecs that could crack walnuts and biceps that made women drool. No, she would not drag the back of her hand across her mouth to check for telltale signs she was doing that now.

"Then why not get to know him better?" Lettie pressed.

"You know his family, his background. That's the perfect guy to have some fun with."

"Guys like that are just fantasies, Let. They're the type who, in olden times, would've been knights, scooping damsels in distress onto white steeds and galloping off into the sunset—whether the damsel liked it or not."

"Wouldn't mind being scooped onto a horse by a guy like Ari Katsalos," Lettie said. "Hell, I'd lie draped over his skateboard if a guy got all knightish on me."

Grace chuckled. "You and I know that guys like Ari Katsalos are controlling and demanding. They're really only interested in what can make them happy, who can make them feel better about themselves." One thing for certain was that they caused her to make bad decisions for herself, and she wanted nothing more to do with them.

"Okay, hun," Lettie said. "You keep on telling yourself that you're going to be able to resist a guy like Ari. That great hunk of manhood? I'll believe it when I see it."

"I'd better go and finish up for the day," Grace said. "Let's meet at the store tomorrow, and we can go over a plan for the week."

Grace ended the call but sat thinking about what Lettie had said. Whenever she'd been around Ari, she could sense his gaze on her, feel his body calling her name, and although in the old days her body would've called right on back before her brain could even register what was happening, now she fought those feelings. This time, things would be different.

Marrying someone who'd had that effect on her, but who'd then controlled every part of her life, had made her swear off the testosterone-plus type like Ari for good.

She and Mark had had incredible chemistry in the beginning, but then the warning signs had begun to appear. He'd tell her what lipstick shade to wear and not to cut her hair because it was frumpy. He started telling her who she should and shouldn't be mixing with. He'd always ask what time she'd be home, and when she got home, he wanted to know who she'd been with. When he'd demanded she stop work because it took her attention away from their life together, she'd known their marriage was over for good. She'd been blind to that side of Mark before she'd married him, and it meant she needed to always be on high alert for people like him—people who had bigger egos than any relationship could sustain and who'd do what it took to get what they wanted.

Next time around, she needed a soul mate, someone dependable and empathetic. A partner. Someone who'd always have her back, but someone who'd give her the freedom to be who she wanted. Next time, she'd recognize that chemical connection to a guy as exactly what it was —danger.

She walked out of her office and across the paved court-yard to the restaurant. The late August sun still burned brightly and reflected the brilliant purple of the bougainvillea against the wedding hall's whitewashed walls. Boris, the cat, lay sprawled on his back in a patch of sun, one paw draped across his eyes as if he was a swimsuit model. It was hard to believe they were in Brentwood Bay. On a day like this, they could be on a Greek island, which was just the atmosphere Mano and Pia had wanted to create when they'd built this place decades ago.

She stopped by Monty's cage and reached into her pocket for a peanut. "*Chronia polla,*" she said in her best parrot voice. The Greek-speaking bird had become a Palace favorite. On cue, he could say *chronia polla*—"many happy years"—to the wedding couple as they strolled past, and according to Mano, some of the younger guests had taught him how to cuss.

*Chronia polla. Chronia polla.* The parrot flew to the side of the cage but didn't take the nut as he usually would.

"Have those workmen been feeding you again?" she said as she scratched his cheek. He fluffed himself out, and she noticed a scattering of feathers on the ground. She'd get someone to clean his cage in the morning. "Looks like I'll be seeing a bit more of you after all, old fella," she said as she stroked the bright green feathers.

Monty stuck his beak through the bars, and she patted it before heading toward the restaurant.

She opened the door and nearly stepped right back out again. Ari was among the tables and chairs in the middle of the room.

On a ladder.

Naked from the waist up.

"Hey," he said, tossing her a grin that shot a bolt of fire through every internal organ. He resumed whatever he was doing to something on the ceiling. "Finishing up soon?"

Her breath stalled. "Soon," she managed as she tried to focus on anything but Ari's perfect abs and his burnished olive skin.

*As soon as I can remember my name and how to start breathing again.*

"Just a couple more things to do." She swallowed, her gaze fixed on the bright tattoo completely covering the upper part of his right arm and spreading onto his chest. His biceps flexed as he screwed in a fitting on the ceiling fan, and the images rippled across his skin. What were they? All she knew was that she had to rip her eyes away.

*Now, how to leave without tripping over anything?*

Clearing her throat, she pretended to rearrange some chairs. "I didn't realize you were here. Theo usually does that sort of thing."

He pulled a T-shirt from where it had been hooked into his jeans and wiped his face, the muscles across his stomach —God help her—rippling with the movement. "We're not spending any money we don't have to. I can fix the fan. How are the weddings for this weekend tracking?"

"I'll open a window," she said, grateful for an excuse to cross to the other side of the room. "Everything's set. I thought you'd be busy at your office downtown."

"Hardly an office," he said. "It's just a temporary bolt-hole, somewhere I can run my agency from while I'm back in the bay."

She opened a latch, pushed the window outward, and breathed in fresh air. "What sort of PI work do you do?"

He finished what he was doing, tucked the T-shirt back into his jeans, and moved down the ladder. "Catch people cheating on their spouse. I thought the city was bad, but my phone's been running red hot since the word got out I'm in town for a while."

He moved closer, and Grace's hormones sat up and begged. Her gaze fixed on the tattoo again—there were brilliant reds, yellows, and blues, a detailed series of figures close together. Were they Greek gods?

*Don't drool. Don't drool.*

Sex on legs didn't come close—he was a walking fantasy.

Grace knew that Mano and Pia hadn't seen much of their eldest son, Nick, over the years, and although they talked about Ari a lot, he hadn't been around much either, except once when he dropped in while Nick was running the place. The time before that, he'd asked her on a date, and if she'd been sane, she'd have said no, but she'd gone through with it. As the evening had gone on, he'd seemed more and more confident, and her skin had become warmer every time he'd looked at her. She'd cut it short to prevent herself doing something she'd regret—like kiss him and never stop.

This morning's horoscope flashed in her mind: *You've worked too hard to be diverted by the charms of temptation. Keep your eyes on the prize. An unexpected disaster will bring endless fortune.*

Yes, if Ari Katsalos was one thing, it was a package of Grade-A temptation, and it appeared he'd been thrown into her path to test her resolve to move on from men like him. Well, it would take more than a godlike body and a few lines of sexy charm to get her to stray from her path. If he was the unexpected disaster, then all she needed to concentrate on was the endless fortune that clearly lay ahead.

She stood tall and moved between the tables, already covered with white tablecloths for the weekend, relieved to see him pulling the T-shirt from the back of his jeans again.

"How often will you be here in the next few weeks?" she asked as she picked up a tray of candles, ready to be placed in the center of the tables.

He gave a small shrug. "Just when you need me, I guess." His phone rang, and he pulled it from his pocket and answered. "Hey, bro."

Grace busied herself with the candles while Ari talked to his brother, Nick, who was visiting their parents in Greece.

"Yep, everything's fine here." He threw her a grin and warmth spread across her cheeks.

There was a long silence before Ari said, "Wow, that's great, but why so soon?"

He nodded at whatever his brother was saying, and Grace moved toward the door to give him some privacy, but he held up a hand to indicate she shouldn't leave. "Yep, she's here. Want to talk to her?"

He paused again and winked at her. An actual, old-fashioned wink. Melting into a puddle on the floor right now was completely possible.

"Okay, let me know when your flight gets in and if there's anything I can do to help get things organized." He paused then laughed loudly. "Yeah, you're right. I was only being polite." Grinning, he passed the phone to Grace. When she held it to her ear, there was a moment's silence before Erin Patterson spoke. They'd gotten to know each other a little when Nick was running the Palace and he and Erin had a wager to win a big contract, but she didn't know her well enough for a special phone call from Greece.

"I was so excited when Ari called last night and told us your news," Erin said. "I know you'll do brilliantly in your own business, and it couldn't have been more perfect timing for me."

Grace sighed quietly in relief. She'd been so worried the Katsalos family would feel she'd let them all down with her decision to leave. "Why's that?"

Ari's gaze was trained on her face, so she had to focus hard on what Erin was saying. She concentrated on a window in the distance.

"We've decided to come home and get married straight away, and I'd love it if you could do the planning for me."

Her heart stopped. Planning the wedding that—because of the much-publicized wager—was going to be the social event of the season? It was almost too much to hope for.

"I…are you sure? I would've thought you'd want to organize it yourself," she heard herself say.

Erin laughed lightly. "The thing is, Nick and I've decided we want to be married as soon as possible, and of course we'll have to have it at Patterson's, so I'm going to need someone on the ground to get things started for me."

"What sort of date were you thinking?"

There was silence, and for a second Grace wondered if they'd been cut off. "Two weeks from Saturday."

She swallowed swiftly as Ari grinned back at her.

"You know," Erin said slowly, "if it's too much for you I completely under—"

"Erin, I'd love to!"

Could she do it? There were two weddings this weekend, and so much stuff to organize for her new business, and she suspected Ari was going to be only slightly more than useless in the organization department. But it could be just the start her new business needed. All the publicity they'd get from *Wedding World*—the magazine who'd covered the wager—she couldn't ask for a better start.

"If I can get Ari to help me around here for the next couple of weeks, then I'm sure we can make things work. Thank you so much for having faith in me."

"Oh, I'm so pleased and, to be honest, relieved. And Nick will be over the moon. He said it just wouldn't be the same without you involved. He wants to take me to Rome on the way home to choose my dress, so I think we'll be home this weekend, but I have all my ideas in an email ready to send to you. My sister Faith will be in touch about a few things, and of course you know Leo really well, so coordinating the food won't be a problem. Oh, Grace, you don't know what it means to me."

After a few more plans and the promise she'd call again tomorrow, Erin said bye and Grace was left standing with the phone in her hand.

"Can you believe it?" she said, her voice breathy. "I knew they were engaged, but I didn't think they'd get married this quickly."

Ari shrugged a shoulder. "What can I say? People lose their heads when it comes to love. It's what keeps bread on my table."

*So cynical.* "Do you think that means your mom and dad will come home?" she said to his back as he folded the ladder.

*We're talking. Actual words. And I can do it without drooling or sounding like an idiot.*

"My mom would sooner walk over hot coals than miss

Nick's wedding, so absolutely they'll be here." He shot her a toe-curling smile.

"You think your parents will be home for good?"

He shrugged. "Don't know. An unexpected wedding to plan is gonna be a lot of extra work for you now, so I'll try and be around as much as possible 'til everyone gets home."

"Oh, I'm sure I'll be fine," she said, switching between panic and elation at the opportunities in front of her. Truthfully, she was starting to wonder how she could manage. Maybe she would need some more help from Ari.

"I can see how important this is, and I want to be here for you," he said as one of his slow, warm smiles lit his face. "I can put a hold on a couple of my cases to spend more time here. Besides, you and me here together? What could possibly go wrong?"

## 2

"Ari, can you call the lighting guy and tell him the spots on the banquet table aren't working? When you've done that, can you ask Polly why the gold ones weren't delivered with the rest of the sugared almonds yesterday, please. Tomorrow's bride said it's a tradition in her family to scatter gold almonds on the tables for good luck, and I'd hate for her to walk in and not see them. She's stopping by this afternoon, so I want to make sure they're here." Grace picked up a stepladder and moved it to one of the columns in the room. "And why does this ribbon keep coming unstuck?" She stabbed at the material with her thumb.

"Let me help," Ari said as he moved closer, impressed by her energy levels—and the fact she could talk so much without taking a breath. As they'd worked together this morning, he'd become increasingly aware of Grace—the way she took charge and made decisions, so organized, and with a spark in her eyes. Sometimes he'd stood where she'd walked just so he could breathe in her floral scent. In quiet moments, he'd catch her scribbling in a notebook or making a phone call to one of her friends, and her face lit up with excitement every time she talked about her new business.

"I've got it," she said and was on the third rung of the ladder before he could reach her. She picked up a piece of ribbon hanging loose and turned back to him. "Can you pass me some of that tape on the table?"

She blinked. He'd never seen such long lashes. They kicked up at the ends and were lush against her olive skin. But the dark smudges under her eyes said she was stressed by all this. He was glad he'd put a few of his cases on hold—it'd mean he could be here a lot more until his family got back.

She turned away, and he ripped a piece of clear tape from a roll on the table. Everything was a blinding sea of white, the only relief the bright red and gold table decorations and large sashes of gold across the main table—and Grace standing on a ladder like a sexy center piece in the middle of it all. A slinky blue top hugged every curve from her full breasts to her rounded hips and finished at the top of pants. Her hair was expertly pinned at the back of her head, not a strand out of place. What he wouldn't give to make it all messy.

He focused on her glossy lips as she turned back and began talking to him again. He handed her the tape. How good would those lips feel under his own.

"Are you listening? Do you remember what I asked you to do?" she asked, smiling as she taped the ribbon into place. "I swear, sometimes I can see you wishing yourself a lobotomy rather than having to deal with all this."

*If she only knew what I was wishing.* He shrugged. "Lights?"

She blew out an exasperated breath. "Scorpios."

"Sorry?"

"You're a Scorpio." She looked down at him. "Your mom

told me about delivering you in a snowstorm just before Thanksgiving."

He grinned. She'd been talking with his mother about him? What else had his mom said? "Not a good star sign for wedding planning, then?"

She bit her lip and studied him. "You like to be involved, but you're not so good on the details or at toeing the line."

"That'd be right." He chuckled. "I'd rather scoop my eyeballs out with a blunt spoon than have to count napkins and polish champagne glasses all day. What sign are you?"

He leaned against the column, now intrigued as all hell by astrology, despite never giving it a second's thought before.

"Libra," she said. "The one with the scales. Trying to make everything balanced and hoping everyone has a great time. Perfect for wedding planning." She finished taping the ribbon and had started down when her foot slipped and the ladder wobbled. He reached out and grabbed her, but when he set her on the floor, he didn't let go.

"I find balance overrated," he said with a grin, and her blue eyes rounded. "Far more fun when things are unpredictable." She smelled of spring flowers and bubble bath, and he held her closer, the bare skin of her arms smooth under his fingers. "Are they a good match, Scorpios and Libras?"

Her lips parted as she started to pull away. "Scorpio and Libra?" She shook her head as she studied his left shoulder. "No. Scorpios have a dark and intense side, and Libras would rather keep things lighter. More realistic. Not a good match at all." She stepped from his grip as a trail of pink swept across her cheek.

"Dark and intense?" Was she referring to a textbook on star signs, or was that how she really saw him? The way she was looking everywhere but directly at him suggested this was her own little personality profile for him, and it set his blood simmering.

"Apparently." She picked up the pen and clipboard from the table and surveyed the room. He could practically see her doing an internal balancing act. She was definitely attracted to him, he was certain of it, but there was some sort of war going on within her. The Scorpio in him was itching to test it.

He rubbed his neck. "I don't know how you do this job. I grew up around weddings, and I don't get the whole drama—bitchy people, who smile together one day and stab each other in the back the next, the crazy expense, the double standards."

Her jaw dropped open. "You don't believe in marriage?"

He shrugged. "Marriage? Hell no. Weddings? Double hell no."

"But the romance of a wedding. Watching people so in love coming together with their families?" Her brow crisscrossed in a frown.

He snorted. "And the tension? The fights? The mothers who can't keep their noses out of things, and the uncles who drink too much."

"Oh, there you are." Polly, one of the restaurant staff, came rushing into the room carrying another clipboard. "We have some major problems."

Grace turned. "What is it?"

"Well, the groom for the nineteenth called to cancel because he's being deployed so they're going to a registry office this afternoon, and the guy from the sugared almond place just called to say the gold almonds for tomorrow's wedding went to the wrong venue. He delivered them to Patterson's last night, and he's busy on the other side of town right now so can't fix the mistake. Don't we need them to show the bride this afternoon?"

Grace put the end of the pen between her lips. "Shoot. If it were anyone else, it'd be easy enough to get them to put the almonds in a cab or something, but I'm never sure how things will go at Patterson's, especially without Erin there. I heard her father's back while she's away."

"Can't you substitute candy or something?" Ari asked, fascinated by her ability to think through every little detail and multitask.

"We have to have those almonds." Grace's frown deepened. "I'm not going to tell the bride her lucky charms aren't here."

Polly put her hands on her hips. "Can't we get them from somewhere else then?"

Grace shook her head. "There's no time. And besides, these have the bride and groom's initials on them. Don't worry, I'll sort it. Polly, can you go and check the outdoor bar?"

Ari pushed himself off the table. "I'll go to Patterson's. If I remember right, the old man can be pretty intimidating." His last memory of Erin's father was when he had Ari's father, Mano, by the collar over a wedding booking they'd both wanted. It was a miracle blood hadn't been spilled. He supposed they were going to be practically family soon—when Nick and Erin were married—so it wouldn't hurt to drop by and introduce himself.

Grace shook her head. "No, you won't. If I'm going to be organizing his daughter's wedding, what better time to show Mr. Patterson I've got things under control." She took out her phone. "I'll get an Uber now."

"An Uber? It won't take long to drive there and back."

She had her cell to her ear. "I don't have a car."

No car? He'd known women living in downtown San Francisco who didn't own a car, but that must be pretty tough in Brentwood Bay. Especially with the sort of job she had.

"Then it makes sense I give you a lift," he said as he reached into his pocket for his keys.

"I didn't know you had a car here."

"I don't. I have a bike."

She hesitated—the war thing happening behind her eyes again. "How can you carry me and a stack of almond boxes?"

"I've carried all sorts of crazy things on my bike," he said. "Once, I had a client who needed me to get back the cat her ex-girlfriend had taken off with. If I can handle a scratching, spitting cat while riding through San Fran traffic, I think we can work something out. Whatever we do, you need to make a decision now."

"I guess." They were running out of time. "We don't really have any choice."

"That's settled then."

Five minutes later, they were in front of his motorcycle in the garage under his parents' apartment. He couldn't remember the last time a woman had ridden on the back of his bike, but the thought of Grace Bennett pressed against his back for the next ten minutes made him wonder why not. "Here, take this," he said, holding out a leather motorcycle jacket he'd found hanging on the wall.

She didn't move. "What for?"

"Because even though it's warm out, it can feel cold when you're riding. It'll give you some sort of protection if you fall off. And"— he smiled—"it's a leather jacket. What's not to love?"

She was still dubious, playing it safe. "I've never been on a motorcycle before. My mom says they're death traps."

He grinned. "I'll take good care of you."

She put her hand on the seat, her face softening. "Been riding long?"

"From the time I could get a license—and even before that. I couldn't wait to get out of here, and when my uncle introduced me to Harleys, it was like I could finally have my freedom." *As far away from playing it safe as I could get.*

She tilted her head. "Why did you want to get out of here so badly?"

His mouth dried, and he moved behind her. When she held out her arm, he guided the jacket sleeve up her arm. Why had he said that? It wasn't something he'd thought about for a long time and not something he discussed with anyone. It made his chest hollow.

"You know, teenage stuff," he said as he drew the jacket around her shoulders.

With the jacket on, Grace stepped out of Ari's hold. When she'd slipped from the ladder and fallen into his strong arms earlier, her breath had died in her lungs. Now she was going to get on the back of a bike and be pressed into that perfectly defined body, and the thought sent goose bumps racing across her skin.

"Whose is it?" she said as she stroked one arm of the jacket

"An old one of mine. Gives you kind of a wild vibe."

"I'm not interested in being wild," she said as she crossed her arms in front. Was that what he had wanted for himself? Was that why he'd left home so young? She stood taller as he picked up another leather jacket and put it on. Taking a deep breath, she tried to force her racing heartbeat to slow. "We don't have much time."

His scent of sea breeze and freshly cut wood seeped into every part of her.

"And you'll need this," he said, picking a red and white helmet off a rack. "Yasmin used to wear it, but I think it'll fit if you take your hair down."

He stepped closer, and her lungs searched for more air. "This will take too long," she said in a fluster. "Maybe I could try calling Erin's sister and get her to send the almonds over. I really shouldn't leave Polly on her own."

He sighed and shook his head. "Polly's fine, and you've got your phone. Let's go."

She moistened her lips.

"Nervous?" He folded his muscled arms across his chest.

"What?" She could barely breathe.

"About being on the back of a bike with me."

She took what she hoped would be a calming breath to move oxygen around her body. "I'd be nervous on the back of a bike with anyone."

He said nothing, but his lips tipped slightly at the corners, and heat blossomed on her neck.

Why, oh, why did he have this effect on her? It made no logical sense, and she had to get herself under control. "Do you know how to get there?"

He blinked. "Of course. Are you taking your hair down?"

He took another step closer, reached up, and pulled the pin from her hair. He kept his dark brown eyes fixed on her face as the waves brushed her cheeks, and the air around them stilled. Every one of her cells jumped to attention.

Her body came alight under his touch, and she fought to keep her reaction under control. *Breathe!*

Gently, he put the helmet on her head and pushed it down.

He fastened the strap under her chin, his gaze like an untamed animal, confident and sure. Was he imagining their bodies pressed close? She swallowed, and then he flipped down her visor, turned, and threw one denim-clad leg over the seat.

He did up his own helmet. "You've got a license, right?" he asked over his shoulder.

She shrugged and tried to make her voice breezy. "Oh, I got a license. I just never got around to getting a car, and now I'm not sure I could remember how to drive. I have a mountain bike, and that gets me where I need to go."

"Going to be tricky running your own business without a vehicle." He fiddled with something up front as she battled with indecision. How should she get on? How close should she sit? And what would his strong body feel like under her fingers? "Meeting clients and suppliers will be difficult," he said, oblivious to her turmoil. He twisted around again. "Hey, maybe I can help you find a car."

She pushed up the leather sleeve of the jacket and looked at her watch. They really didn't have much time.

"Okay, we're going," he said, misinterpreting her indecision. He grabbed the handlebars and started the machine. The Harley came to life, and the air around them was filled with the deep rumble of the engine. "You can get on now," he said over his shoulder.

Grace hesitated.

This was a test, just as this week's horoscope had said. She couldn't help the way she was wired—the way the sexually charged parts of her body and brain fired first. But she wasn't going to let that side of her dominate anymore. All sorts of mischief was brewing in Ari's sinful, dark eyes, and she'd resist it at every turn.

Of course, she could touch a man like Ari and have nothing come of it. She chewed the inside of her lip.

*Just do it.*

*He's so hot.*

"Are you getting on?" he asked again.

She lifted one leg over the bike and grabbed hold of him to steady herself. Her hands met his strong shoulders before she got control. Her mouth dried, and she had to take a minute for her pulse to stop racing.

When she was settled behind him, he reached back and grabbed her wrist then wrapped her arm around his waist "Hold me tight around here. And scoot forward a little. The closer we are, the better the balance. And when we go around a corner, just lean the way I lean. We need to move together."

Scared of what her body might do when it was flush against Ari's, she took a second to compose herself.

Placing her other arm around his waist, she breathed in his scent. A new mix of freshly laundered cotton, rich nutty leather, and strong, warm male assaulted her senses, and her whole body came alive. His jacket was open at the front, and under the black cotton T-shirt was rock-hard torso, his warmth bleeding into her fingers as they flattened on his abs.

*Stupid body. Behave.*

"Okay?" he called over the roar of the engine.

"Yes," she breathed as the bike sprang to life under her, and they were moving out onto the street. The vibrations from the engine were a deep buzz between her legs. How in God's name had she ended up squeezed tight against Ari like this?

As he swerved around a parked car, she squeezed her knees into his thighs and instinctively hugged him tighter. She marveled at the shape of him under his jacket, the power in his legs as they gripped the bike, and she couldn't help but imagine being under him, wrapped in those powerful arms, his body providing the vibrations for hers.

And a fantasy was fine. There was absolutely nothing wrong with imagining a guy like Ari Katsalos taking her to bed and fulfilling every twisted wish she'd ever had. She could imagine him kissing his way down her. It was okay to think about opening herself to him, to dream about him making love to her…

*As long as it stays a fantasy.*

Heat rolled through her, and she sat a little straighter. Fantasies and dreams were fine, harmless fun, but that was all she could have with a guy like Ari now. Of course, sex and sexual attraction were vital parts of a relationship, but they wouldn't be what defined a partnership for her anymore.

*You're strong. And smart. You will not give in to whatever the hell this is.*

He tilted his head back. "Everything okay back there?"

She watched as his fingers closed again around the handlebars, and she dreamed about him running his rough hands up her thighs. "Mmm-hmm," she managed.

But it so wasn't.

Ari pulled his bike up in front of the impressive black iron gates of Patterson's weddings, killed the engine and placed his feet on the ground. He'd said nothing more to Grace as they'd woven through the streets of Brentwood Bay, but every now and then he'd heard the sharp little intake of breath when they'd swerved to miss a driver opening his car door, or when he'd changed gear to go a little faster.

Grace climbed off the bike as quickly as she could, brushing down the legs of her trousers.

"Like that?" he asked as he undid his helmet.

"Not really." Her tone was tighter than he was used to. "I don't know how you ever keep your clothes clean when you ride out in the open like that." She tugged at the helmet fastening. "And I'm sweating underneath this."

He took her helmet and locked it with his bike. "I'm sorry if I scared you."

"You didn't scare me." She pulled down the zip on her jacket. "I was just wondering why you would want to use that as a way to get around."

"Freedom." He began to follow her to the gate. "I like the solitude of it."

"I bet it's great for all the women you date."

He smiled. "You're the first." He opened the gate for her. "Grace, we should probably clear the air about the last date we went on."

"The only date we went on." She stared straight ahead, but her cheeks were flushed.

He grinned again. "Yeah, that's the one. I did try to call you the next day, you know. And I'm sorry if you thought I was too pushy. Yasmin told me about your divorce and—"

"My divorce had nothing to do with it." Her words were clipped. Maybe he shouldn't have brought this up. "Sorry I didn't call you back." She spoke a little more quickly than usual. "I just felt we weren't right for each other, and there was no point in pretending otherwise."

Punch. To. The. Gut.

He cleared his throat. "How could you know so quickly we weren't right for each other? And besides, it was only dinner. I wasn't asking you to run away with me."

She blinked. "I thought it was pretty obvious there wouldn't have been a future for us. We live in different towns, have different lifestyles."

"Are you telling me you only date guys you can imagine walking down the aisle with?"

She kept moving, but he could tell by the tight set of her shoulders that he'd hit a pretty big nerve.

"You can't be serious," he said as he lengthened his stride to catch up. "You only want to spend time with guys you can see yourself married to?"

"This really isn't the right time to be discussing this," she said as she went up to the door and pressed the bell. "But for your information, no, I don't, but life's too busy to spend all my time kissing frogs. A guy at least has to have the right temperament to be my prince, or there's no point in taking things further." Her eyes sparked.

He stared at her as she turned back to face the door. Temperament? She didn't like his *temperament*?

No way. He'd seen the way she looked at him, and she probably hadn't noticed how she rubbed her hands against his abs when they were on the bike.

He had.

She didn't want to admit she was attracted to him, and he burned to know why.

The door opened, and Grace was back in her business mode. "Hi, I'm Grace from the Aegean Palace," she said to the smiling woman. "You have a delivery that should've been for us?"

"Oh yes," the woman said and then turned and held out her hand to Ari. "Hi, I recognize you. I'm Faith Patterson. I believe we're going to be family soon?"

"Ari Katsalos," Ari said as he shook Faith's hand and returned her smile. "And sooner than any of us imagined."

"We're thrilled to be hosting Erin and Nick's wedding and really pleased it can be a joint effort with you doing the planning, Grace." Faith gestured inside. "Would you like to come in?"

"No, thanks," Grace said, resuming her normal, chatty tone. "I'm afraid we need to get back for an appointment this afternoon, but I'd love to come by tomorrow and talk through some of the plans with you, if that suits."

Faith smiled again. "Sounds perfect. I'll just grab your package."

When she'd gone, Grace turned to Ari, a determined tilt to her chin. "Given that most of your family will be back here in the next week or so, why don't you just leave things to me? It doesn't make sense to be involved in something you really don't know anything about. I'm sure I'll be fine on my own."

She didn't want him at the Palace because she didn't trust herself around him.

"I want to do my bit for my family," he said. "I haven't been around much lately, and having my parents in Greece for so long... Maybe I should have been around more. We need to clear the air so we can move forward."

Faith arrived back with the package, they said their good-byes, and then Grace turned and headed back up the driveway.

"What is it you're worried about?" Ari asked as he followed her. He'd never met a woman who pretended so hard she wasn't attracted to him. "That I'll distract you? I'll get in your way?"

*That I'll want to kiss you every time I see you?* It was true. He'd thought of little else this last week.

She stopped and turned to face him. "My life is jam-packed, and I don't have any time to play games. It would be unfair to pretend differently."

"So, you're *not* attracted to me?" He raised his eyebrows. "Or you don't have *time* to be attracted to me?"

She did the sexy little lip rub thing he'd noticed she did whenever she got flustered. "I was married to someone who had chemistry off the charts with me." She paused and pulled in a breath. "Dangerously so, and it made me do stupid things. I want something different now."

A small muscle tightened in her cheek.

"One second," he said, trying to hide his shock at what she seemed to be suggesting. "You mean the next person you have a relationship with, you don't want to be attracted to? How does that even work? And why not just have some fun with someone when you find you like them?"

This time the skin on her cheeks turned scarlet, and it was the most beautiful thing he'd seen in a very long time. "I'm flattered, really, I am," she said, "but under the circumstances, I think it's best if we focus on our own priorities. I panicked when Erin asked me to plan their wedding. You don't need to be here anymore.

He blew out a hot breath. "So now you're saying you can't work with me?"

She rubbed her hand up and down her neck. "Yes, I guess that's what I mean." She cleared her throat and held his gaze. "I'm sorry, Ari." She held out her hand as if to shake his, but he ignored it. They were waaaay past the hand-shaking stage.

He paused, trying to find the words to bring back the sparkling, open Grace he'd seen in the past. "If that's the way you feel."

She nodded. "I think it's for the best."

He shrugged. "Well, I've hired my office space in town now, and I may as well stay around until Nick and Erin's wedding. I just want you to promise me one thing."

She blinked. "Which is?"

"If you do need me, you'll put aside your feelings and give me a call."

"I don't think that's going to be necessary," she said. "And if it's all the same to you, I'll be getting an Uber back to the Palace."

3

On Monday afternoon, Grace fell into her office chair, breathed deeply, and stared at the planner on her desk. If she could get someone to pick up the imitation swans from the accessory store before three, then she could get to the cake shop by four and be back here by half past, in time to send an email with the last of the table decoration proposals off to Erin, ready for a decision by the morning. Maybe then she'd have time to do the rosters for tomorrow.

It hadn't been easy, but she'd been pretty pleased with the way she was managing by herself since the talk with Ari. It was kind of like going on a diet, really. If the big old chocolate cake with fudge frosting and fresh cream in the middle wasn't staring at you from the refrigerator, it was much easier to put the thought of indulging in it completely out of your mind.

*Except when you're constantly dreaming of licking the frosting.*

The ride on his motorcycle that day had only confirmed she couldn't control her thoughts when she was around him, so the only way to fix that was to stop seeing him completely. And although she might've dreamed about him once or twice, and maybe even noticed her ears straining when one of his family members mentioned him, she was just focusing on finishing here so she could run her own business.

*No more temptation.*

The landline rang, and she considered not answering. If it was something else to squeeze into her day, she didn't quite know how she would manage it. Her OCD tendencies overpowered her, though, and she picked up the handset.

"The Aegean Palace, Grace Bennett speaking."

"Ari Katsalos, please."

The male voice on the other end was sharp and brusque. But the fact she could hear Ari's name without her pulse spiking might mean progress.

"I'm sorry, Mr. Katsalos isn't working at the Palace any longer. Perhaps I can help?"

The man sighed heavily. "And you are?"

"Grace Bennett, wedding planner."

"Right, you'll do," the voice said with barely hidden irritation. "It's Congressman Williams here. I'm sure you'll have heard about my daughter's wedding—the magazine stories and all that."

"Absolutely," Grace said, puzzled as to why he'd be calling here when Erin had won the wager against Nick, meaning Amy Williams's wedding was to be held at Patterson's next year. There'd been a lot in the papers recently about some kind of scandal with the congressman, but she hadn't followed it properly. "We were pleased to be able to compete to hold Amy's wedding, but we're sure everything will go well at Patterson's."

"That's the thing," the congressman said. "My daughter's wedding is going to be sooner than expected, and Patterson's can't accommodate us anymore. They don't seem to appreciate the significance of their decision, but believe me, they'll regret it."

"Oh, I see. I'd understood it was planned for next July?" Grace had already flicked to the Palace's online booking calendar and was madly scrolling to July.

"Yes, well, now we need it to be held next Saturday, the nineteenth."

Next week! Reality dawned. Patterson's wouldn't be able to hold the Williams wedding there because it was Erin and Nick's date. "You mean you'd like us to host it here?"

"I wouldn't want any corners cut. There's an exclusive deal with a national publication for photos, and there will be dignitaries coming from overseas. My daughter always said she preferred your food, but I'm not going to pay for some second-rate offering in terms of venue or service. If we hold it at your place, then I expect the very best of everything."

Grace's heart pounded. Not only would she get to plan Erin and Nick's wedding, she would be responsible for this one too. Could she do it? All sorts of implications rushed through her mind. That this could finally be the saving grace for Pia and Mano. That being responsible for two of the most high-profile weddings of the year could be an incredible springboard for her own business. That there was no way on God's green Earth she could do all of this on her own...

"I need an answer now," the congressman said. "You're either in or you're out."

Grace flicked pages in the planner and her eyes raced over the pages for next week. She couldn't ask Meg and Lettie to help—they were in LA at an enormous bridal expo and wouldn't be back until Monday the twenty-first.

There was a vow renewal set for Friday afternoon, but she was pretty sure she could move it outside or maybe even earlier, in which case the reception hall would be free, but she had rehearsals to run at Patterson's, not to mention the entire Katsalos family returning from Greece... But then she remembered the cancelled wedding, so there was an opening. Maybe this could be the fortune her horoscope had mentioned! "We'll do it," she said in a rush. "I'll send the contracts through to your office this evening—"

"My daughter will be in touch," the congressman said across her. "And if any media contact you in the meantime, you're to say it's been brought forward due to my daughter's schedule. No other reason. Understood?"

Before she had time to answer, the congressman hung up, and she was left staring at the phone, her hands shaking and her mind sprinting. She couldn't physically be in two places at once. And each of these weddings was going to have to be planned down to the last piece of confetti. She put her elbows on the desk and speared her fingers through her hair.

There was really only one person who knew how important these two weddings were to the Palace. Only one person who could help her manage the return of the Katsalos family in the next few days and have a cool enough head to help her run things smoothly. Now that Amy Williams's wedding was to be held here, it could mean a complete turnaround in fortune for Mano and Pia Katsalos. And for their children, too. She shouldn't try and shoulder this alone when Ari had said he'd be there to help if she needed him...

Before she let the little devil on her shoulder change her mind, she picked up her phone and scrolled through her contacts. Damn. On impulse, she'd deleted Ari's number the day she'd told him she wouldn't be needing him here anymore. Remembering he'd given her a card the first day he was here, she flicked through the papers on her desk until she found it, perched precariously on the edge.

She dialed the number, and when it went to voicemail, she left a message. "Ari, something major has come up, and I'm going to need your help."

~

After getting out of the Uber, Grace stood on the pavement outside Ari's office and let her hand hover above the door-bell. If he was any decent sort of a human being, he'd have replied to the three messages she'd left on his phone this morning. But he hadn't. And yet, he'd said he'd be there when she needed him.

*Where the hell is he?*

She pressed the buzzer—hard. He might be the black sheep of the family, but it didn't mean he couldn't have some manners. Maybe he'd gone back to the city? She'd made it clear she was happier working far away from him, so it'd make sense if he'd left Brentwood Bay all together.

"Yeah." His voice was sharp and hard.

"Ari, it's me, Grace."

"Oh, right. Sorry, I was expecting someone else."

"I need to talk to you urgently," she said, wishing she could keep her voice steady.

There was silence for a moment. "Now's not a great time," he said. "Can I call you?"

She'd come across town to speak to him, and he was going to blow her off? "I've come all the way over here, so I'd really like to speak to you now. It's important."

He hesitated. "Okay, come up."

When it buzzed, she pushed the door open and made her way along a dimly lit corridor. When she was nearly at the end, a door opened, and Ari stood there.

He wore shorts and a black T-shirt, half tucked in, half hanging loose. His hair, never styled much, stood at all sorts of angles as if he'd been sleeping on it for hours.

"Why haven't you been returning my calls?" She didn't mean to sound so abrupt, but maybe she'd interrupted him with a woman. How could she have been so stupid? Of course, that's why he hadn't been calling her. She'd practically told him she didn't want to have anything more to do with him, and he'd moved on. She instinctively took a step back.

*Why am I hoping that's not true?*

"Hey, I'm sorry. I pulled an all-nighter and must've fallen asleep at my desk." He scrubbed a hand through his hair, and she noticed he had bare feet. "You want coffee?"

"An all-nighter?" Did he mean he was with a woman all night? That he'd been partying?

"Yeah, but I finally got the information I need on this guy I've been following, so it was worth it."

He stood aside and gestured for her to come in.

She let out a private sigh of relief that she hadn't made a complete fool of herself.

"Do you have your bike?" he asked, looking past her.

"No, I caught an Uber. Ari, things have gone a bit crazy at the Palace."

"Really? If you want you can have a coffee while I take a shower, then I'll drive you back. Maybe you can tell me what's happening on the way."

She should be ashamed of herself. Here was a guy, not only trying to help his parents out but trying to maintain his own business at the same time, and she'd thought the worst of him. "Okay, thanks," she said as she moved into the room.

"Sorry, things are a bit temporary here," he said as he closed the door behind her.

She stepped into a brightly lit warehouse, basically an enormous room with a kitchen and bed side by side. Well, she assumed it was a bed. It was in the shape of one but was hidden beneath a pile of clothes and various boxes with paper hanging out of them.

"So, you're living here as well as using it as an office?"

He moved past her and around behind the counter.

He nodded. "I figured between keeping an eye on the Palace and running my PI work from here, I wouldn't be at home much, so this is the best of both worlds. Luckily, there's a bathroom, but nowhere to wash clothes, so I need to make a trip to the laundromat."

She surveyed the room. *A laundromat or a front-end loader.* Even what he was using as a kitchen counter had packets stacked up and at least half a dozen cups spread across it. Her fingers itched to pick up the newspaper that was strewn across the floor, but she folded her arms instead.

"As you can see, I wasn't expecting company," he said, but he made no attempt to pick anything up. "Just dump that pile of clothes off the stool there and have a seat."

She stayed where she was, determined to get out of here as quickly as she could. The thought of picking up a whole pile of clothes with his scent was too much. "I'm fine, thanks." When Ari moved into the kitchen, something caught her eye. Bits of paper, like those ripped from a school exercise book, were pinned on the walls. Were they receipts? Interview questions?

She moved forward to take a better look, but he spoke again, and she turned back to him.

"I'm sorry I haven't been picking up calls," he said over his shoulder, "but there's this guy I've been tailing for three weeks, and yesterday I finally found something that could close the case. Sometimes you've just got to strike when you can."

"What sort of a guy?" She imagined a big shot executive cheating on his wife.

Ari pulled two coffee cups from a cupboard as he continued. "This woman who travels a lot for her job suspects her husband's been having an affair. She's even built it up to imagining he has a whole new family in another state, so I've been running an investigation for the past couple of months."

"And what did you find?"

"That she's right. He is having an affair, and although he doesn't have a whole new family, he's setting things up to move out when the time's right. I haven't told her what I've found yet, but none of it'll be a surprise for her. All I really need to seal the deal is some photographic evidence, and when my guy Rick can track him down to a particular location, I'll get it done."

"Maybe they grew apart," Grace said as Ari turned to the refrigerator. She took her chance to look more closely at one of the pieces of paper on the wall. Was it a poem?

The piece was typed, but certain words were underlined. Did he write poems? Somehow the image of the tattooed biker didn't fit with someone who wrote poetry in his spare time. She decided to check it out properly when he was in the shower.

He shrugged. "Could be any number of reasons. I don't really focus on that. My goal is just to catch them."

"What made you choose this sort of work?" She moved toward the counter again. "It must be pretty depressing," she said. How in the hell could someone make disheveled look so sexy?

He shrugged a strong shoulder. "The guaranteed nature of the business," he said. "People are always going to cheat. It's in most people's DNA. I figure running a business where the work is never going to dry up is smart."

She chuckled. "It's kind of ironic, you doing that sort of work and your parents owning a wedding hall."

He turned and poured coffee into two cups. Raising his eyebrows, he said, "I guess you've already figured, or at least my mom would've told you, I'm the black sheep of the family. I've never really followed the Katsalos rules."

Her cheeks heated as she tried to pretend she hadn't talked to Pia about her son. "You obviously care a lot about your family, and I'm sure they support you in what you do," she said, wanting him to open up about himself but not wanting to seem too nosy.

"We never really talk about it," he said. "I think now that my parents are having their own marriage issues, their belief in the wedding and marriage fantasy has taken a bit of a hit."

"But theirs is only a hiccup, surely." Grace couldn't bear the thought of Mano and Pia splitting up. Sure, their relationship was fiery at times, but there was no doubt they loved each other deeply. It was the strain of the business that had caused Pia to leave for Greece. "And now with both your sister and brother getting married…"

He rubbed a hand over his stubbled chin, looking like a magazine model for expensive cologne. "Now I'll be even more of the odd one out."

Sparks burned under her skin. "But you must see that both Yasmin and Nick are really happy, that they'll have great marriages."

He pushed one of the cups toward her. "I certainly think everyone who gets married believes that in the beginning. What about you?" he asked, clearly changing the subject. "Any brothers and sisters?"

"One brother, Luke," she said.

"Married?"

She rolled her lip between her teeth. Saying the word out loud always gave her a sense of failure, but there was no point pretending. His mother had probably told him what a basket case she'd been when she split from Mark. "Divorced, like me. My parents have been married forty years, so it's kind of a disappointment to them that neither of our marriages worked."

He held her gaze, and for a terrible moment she thought he was going to ask about her marriage. For some crazy reason, she didn't want her divorce to be a confirmation of his cynicism. Instead, she had a powerful urge to tell him he was wrong, that there was true love and commitment in the world, that not all husbands or all wives cheated, and that love could be strong and everlasting. And she would've told him, if she wasn't standing in his kitchen in front of his rumpled perfection, his sleepy grin making her stomach flip-flop.

And if she was 100 percent sure of it all herself.

Now was not the time to be talking about the differences between them. "The reason I wanted to get hold of you so urgently," she said, "is that I'm going to need your help. And a lot of it."

He took a mouthful of coffee and swallowed, mesmerized her with the way his throat moved. "Oh, yeah?"

The tension in the room shifted. "I had a call from Congressman Williams, and he wants his daughter's wedding held at the Palace the weekend after next." How she said the words without her head exploding was a mystery.

Ari dug around on a shelf and brought out a bag of sugar. "But wasn't that what the wager was about? Patterson's won the right to hold the event, and that was the end of it? Why did everyone go to all that trouble if they were going to have it at the Palace anyway? Sugar?" he offered. "Sorry it's not in a bowl or anything."

"That's what was supposed to happen, but with Erin and Nick deciding to come back and marry so soon, combined with Amy Williams's wedding being brought forward, every-thing's changed."

Ari dug a spoon into the bag and proceeded to stir two spoonsful into his coffee. "I bet it has something to do with the sexual harassment scandal going on in the congressman's office. A perfect way to deflect from that would be to have photos of him—the doting father—giving away his daughter at her wedding."

"Maybe," she said. "But the bottom line is I'm going to need your help. And I mean all day and half the night if I'm going to make this happen in fourteen days."

"You're sure?" he said, his gaze steady on her. "After what you said at Patterson's that day, I wouldn't think I'd be your first choice."

She picked up her coffee and blew on it, thankful to look anywhere but into his sexy eyes.

"There's no time to get anyone else in," she said, trying not to sound desperate. "You care about making sure this works, and more importantly, you can keep your family out of the way so we can make it happen. I'll call your parents and let them know about the Williams wedding, and then you can keep them updated after that."

Ari nodded. "I hear you about keeping my family in check. Mom will want to be all over Nick's wedding, and she'll be racing around trying to organize all the guests coming from overseas. Okay," he said. "I've got a pretty light load after I finish this one case, so let's do it. We'll make this work together. What say I take a quick shower, and then I give you a lift back to the Palace."

She bit her lip.

"Or if you don't like the back of my bike, we could get an Uber," he said with a grin.

"Great," she said, and he turned and walked into the bathroom.

As soon as she heard the shower running, Grace moved from the counter and took in the rest of the apartment. Because he was only here temporarily, it made sense that Ari didn't have many personal things around. Apart from the piles of clothes, the boxes of papers, a jacket thrown over the back of a chair, and a large overnight bag in the corner, there didn't seem to be anything personal at all. Except the pieces of paper stuck to the wall. She shouldn't really be snooping, but if she was to work closely with him, she needed to be sure he was everything he said he was, didn't she? And apart from anything else, she was curious about what made him tick.

Making sure the door to the bathroom was closed, she moved to the wall by the bed. She almost stood on a phone with two ear pods balanced on top, but she stepped around them and leaned closer.

This piece was typed out like a poem. As she read through it, she realized it was an Ed Sheeran song, and words like *mysterious, beating,* and *thousand* had been underlined. The same words were written underneath in blue pen. The next words were *never, please, forever.*

Maybe the pages had been stuck there by a previous tenant? Even if they had been, why would someone like Ari keep them around? No, he must have put them there himself.

She moved to another piece of paper and found more typed words with the same things written underneath—*dear, love, always, birthday.*

*Okay, so stop right there.* Her brain, which was beginning to compile an inventory of questions to ask Ari. This was not someone to get to know better; this was a man whose help she needed for the next few weeks at the most. The fact he had pieces of poems or song lyrics stuck to his wall shouldn't make him any more interesting than he already was.

But it did, dammit.

Why had there been no sign of this side of him when they'd had that disastrous date?

The water turned off in the shower, and as she swung back toward the counter, her foot nudged the phone and words appeared on the screen. So, he liked books as well? She was dying to find out what it was. *Catcher in the Rye,* maybe, or some other classic? The absolute improbability of that caused the familiar rush she got when she was with him to come racing back. Behind the bathroom door, he'd be stepping out of the shower right now, his olive skin glistening with water droplets, his biceps flexing as he rubbed his body dry. His glossy black hair would be falling damp around his cheek bones…

*What's wrong with you? Just say no to the hot guy.*

She bit her lip again and moved back to the counter.

When he finally emerged from the bathroom, Ari was dressed in a white T-shirt and blue jeans. "Sorry I took so long," he said as he dragged a hand through his damp hair. "Let's go."

She hesitated. How must he be feeling about her change of mind on this? Going back to the Palace when he thought he'd been free of it? She hadn't really considered him, but he'd immediately said yes to her.

"What's up?"

She played with the cuff of her blouse. "I guess you were when I said I didn't need you at the Palace. I know you haven't had much to do with the place over the years."

He shrugged a shoulder. "I was home for Easter. Sometimes Christmas."

"But not regularly like Nick and Yasmin." Was that too pointed?

Ari reached for the jacket on the back of the chair. "What you're really asking is what happened between me and my parents that makes me the black sheep?"

Heat rose on her cheeks. Her interest had been a little too obvious so soon after their earlier conversation. Ari was a private investigator and probably used to people who didn't always tell the truth.

"I guess they didn't know what to make of me," he said with a shrug. "Or what to do for me. As immigrants, their whole lives were geared toward giving their kids opportunities, but even more than that, they desperately wanted their children to have high-status careers, and from a very early age they knew I wasn't going to follow that path."

The flatness in his eyes pulled at something deep within her, and although one part of her brain said a guy like Ari was nothing more than trouble, a primal part wanted to step closer, to narrow the breach and really get to know him.

"You're just the sort of person they relate to," he said. "Someone in a respectable job. Someone with a good background and nothing standing in their way."

He took a step toward her and picked his keys up off the counter. She cursed herself for putting up so many barriers and for the insatiable need to know him a whole lot better.

"So, what was it?" she asked. "They didn't like you writing poetry? They were threatened by your creativity?"

He frowned, and she pointed to the pieces of paper on the wall. "You write lyrics? Study poetry?"

His eyes widened, and he shook his head, an ironic smile on his face. "You really don't know? My mother didn't confide her greatest shame to you?"

Grace shook her head slowly as her heart rate quickened. Had she got it all wrong? "I don't understand what you mean."

Ari laughed, a short, sharp noise holding more pain than joy. "I can't read properly," he said matter-of-factly. "I was diagnosed with severe dyslexia, and after that I had to find a different path than my parents would've chosen."

"Oh, Ari, I'm sorry for snooping," she said. "I didn't mean to—" She burned to take a step toward him, to soothe this beautiful man.

He put the keys in his jacket pocket and lifted his gaze to her. "I've never really succeeded in my parents' eyes. As soon as I could leave home, I took my bike and rode as far as I could and worked in pizza joints 'til I could put myself through police college. Even then, I failed at just about everything in the beginning. An old detective who'd had similar issues to me helped me cram for my final exam. I passed, but eventually it became too difficult to hide that I couldn't fill out paperwork properly, so I got out of the force as soon as I could, took the skills that sort of work had given me, and I've been my own boss ever since."

Grace dropped her head, hating herself for jumping to conclusions about him, so sorry he'd had to face such struggles in his life, and sad that he thought he was a disappointment to his family.

His hand rested on the countertop, and she reached out and touched it. "Your family would be incredibly proud of you right now," she said. "Putting your own life on hold to make sure their business was safe."

He didn't move his hand, and his gaze was fixed on hers. "My family won't have high expectations of me, but that's okay," he said, his features unmoving. "I've never done anything they've been truly proud of, nothing they really value. In lots of ways, they're like you in that they think I'm nothing more than a rough guy with a bike, with no cares and no responsibilities. I get why they feel that way."

She swallowed and dropped her gaze for a moment, and her heart beat deep in her chest.

"Ari, I'm sorry," she said. "That's not the way I meant it."

He laughed, but it sounded forced. "It's okay. Most of the time that's exactly what I'm like, but that's just because it's easier. My family don't expect a lot from me, and I've learned not to expect a lot from them. I've found it works that way."

Her gaze swung to his face. His eyes were as brown as toasted almonds, and when he smiled it lit his features. He might have a tough shell, but for the first time, she could see a softness in him. Her hand was still over his, and she squeezed. "A tough guy wouldn't put his life on hold to help out his family's business, or agree to help someone who'd blown him off not once, but twice. Thank you."

He smiled at her, the tiniest of dimples cutting into his cheeks. "If there's so much work to be done at the Palace, then we should get started."

4

Back at the Palace that afternoon, Ari watched while Grace filled in an enormous planner sheet on the wall of her office. Each day had a long list of bullet points attached, and big stars circled Saturday the nineteenth, the day of both Amy Williams's wedding at the Palace and Erin and Nick's wedding at Patterson's. Beside different entries, she had a color-coded system for who should be in charge of what.

He'd always known she was organized and efficient, but the drive she'd shown in getting this done had exhausted him just watching her.

"Oh, shoot," she said and put the end of the pen between her teeth.

He studied her as she stared at the wall, her gaze flicking up and down, her forehead crumpled the same way it had been when she'd told him at Patterson's that she couldn't work with him—that a bit of fun was something she couldn't consider with him. "I haven't put you in," she said.

"Sorry?" He pulled his attention from her lips to what she was actually saying.

"I didn't factor in that you'll be in the wedding party for Nick and Erin, and I've given you all these jobs to do. Now I'll have to find someone else to help with this stuff." She swung back to him, and he had to focus even harder on what she was saying. As she looked at him, her eyes sparkling, a fizz powered through his blood.

"I can be at Patterson's for Nick and Erin's ceremony and back here for whatever needs to be done after that," he said. "No problem."

She tapped the pen on her chin. "But you'll be in the wedding party, won't you?"

"You mean like best man or groomsman?" He shook his head. "No. Nick has his friends from university. He'll have Lane as his best man, I guess."

A pink flush worked across her cheeks, and she became even more radiant. "Oh, I just assumed…"

"It's fine," he said, feeling her embarrassment. It was natural for her to think he'd be involved in his brother's wedding party, but that's not what his brother would want, and not what Ari would expect. "Nick wants the Palace to succeed as much as I do. He'll be pleased I'm helping out here."

"And how much involvement will your parents want to have when they're back? I guess I should talk to them about how I manage the congressman's daughter's wedding. Since it's such a big deal, maybe they'll want to have a say in what's happening. But then again, they'll be so focused on Nick's wedding." Her face showed genuine concern. "I'm not sure how I feel about running things with them back here."

"I'm not sure what they're expecting," Ari said. "I haven't spoken to them in a while. Mom's always happier if she feels like she's part of the decisions, though."

"Okay," she said, her eyes brightening. "What's the time in Greece right now? Your mom and dad are still not living in the same place, are they? We could call your mom, or even FaceTime her?"

He looked at his watch. He preferred to be prepared when he spoke to his parents, especially his mother. "Ten in the evening. Maybe it would—"

"Is that too late?"

"It's not late for Greece, I guess," he said slowly. "She'll be sitting around talking with my aunt and uncle after dinner. She'll be surprised to hear from me."

She flicked open her computer. "All the more reason why we should call her. I've spoken to her a couple of times since she's been away, but it will be lovely to see her face-to-face." They waited while the computer connected, and then Pia Katsalos's face filled the screen.

"Grace!" Ari heard his mother shriek. "It's so lovely to see you. Maria and I were just sitting here on the computer looking at mother-of-the-groom dresses, and then your beautiful face pops onto my screen. How are you doing? There's so much responsibility for you now, running things while none of us are there, and now there's Nicky's wedding for you to cope with as well. I'm going to be with you in two days, and I will be there to help out with everything. You don't need to worry anymore."

Grace started to speak, but as was typical for his mom, Pia carried right on talking. "And Nicky tells me that Ari has not stayed to help you, which I am very disappointed about." She sighed dramatically. "That boy never seems—"

"Pia, Ari's right here with me," Grace said across his mother as she turned the screen toward him. Ari held Grace's gaze for a moment, and when she gave him the softest of smiles, a depth of understanding passed between them.

It wasn't that he and his mother fought; he just found it difficult being around her, and she often made it clear that she couldn't understand him or his lifestyle. She had a tendency to believe life was simple, that every decision was black and white, right or wrong.

"Hey, Mom," he said, raising a hand. "How's everything in Lesvos?"

"Oh, you are there," his mother said. "I hope you're helping Grace and not getting in her way. We want to have everything perfect for these weddings, and Grace will have it all under control. Make sure you do what she tells you to. It's so important for all of us that this goes smoothly."

He ignored the lecture. "Have you spoken to Dad about when he's coming back?"

His mother blinked, and her features slackened for the briefest moment. "No. I believe from your Uncle Yiannis that your father will be coming for the wedding, but I know nothing more. I will come and stay with you at the Palace, Ari, but your father will need to find somewhere else."

So, obviously a lot of tension still existed between his parents. He'd hoped with the news of Yasmin and Lane getting married, and then Erin and Nick's wedding, as well as a visit from them, that his parents might have overcome some of their differences. Apparently not, and that could mean some strained family get-togethers in the next two weeks. Grace would need his help to keep a cap on that.

"I'm not staying here, Mom. I've rented something in town so I can carry on my own work. I'm here to help Grace whenever she needs me."

His mother was quiet for a moment—a sure sign something was eating at her. She hated what he did for a living, but she hated even more that he had a life of his own away from the tight-knit Greek community in Brentwood Bay.

"It's working out fine," Grace added cheerily, before his mother could object. "I originally thought I could do this all on my own, but now with the Williams wedding, it's great to have Ari's help. I don't need him on site all of the time, but he's been fantastic."

Why was she tripping over herself to stick up for him?

"Well, if you say so," Pia said, still looking dubious.

"So, you can have your place while you're back," Ari said. "That is, unless you've decided to come back permanently."

His mother rubbed her cheeks with her palms. "Let's just say, we will see what happens," she said. "I don't want to have to think about anything other than that the first, and soon the second, of my children will be married. Everything else can be forgotten for now."

They carried on talking for a while then said good-bye and ended the call. When Grace closed the laptop, Ari let out a long breath. The knowledge his parents were still apart cut deep. He might not have always appreciated them, or what they'd done for him, but they'd always been in these buildings, solid and sure, and the fact they were no longer here made him feel more rudderless than usual. Maybe he could talk to his father alone when he was back…

Grace reached out and touched his arm. His blood ran warmer, and his pulse beat directly beneath where she touched him.

She stood, but her hand stayed resting on his arm. "This is pretty hard for you." Her voice was soft and sincere.

He lifted his chin, and the concern on her face knocked him off center. Her understanding seeped deep inside, and he had to stop himself from touching her in return.

"If there's one thing I've learned in the past few years," he said, "it's that relationships can be complicated, especially those between a mom and her children. Mom means well, but she struggles to show it sometimes."

Her voice hadn't held pity, only tenderness and understanding, and he pulled himself up to his full height and stepped forward. "My family owes you an incredible debt,

Grace. And not only for what you've done in the running of this place. You've also helped our family hang together."

Her smile was uncertain. "What do you mean?"

"My brother, my sister, and I had all left home, gotten on with busy lives, but you were here helping our parents when we should've been."

"I'm not sure I did a great job," she said. "Maybe if I'd been more aware, I could've helped your mom through a difficult time and she might not have felt the need to leave."

He shook his head. "No, most people I know would've run a mile if they'd been faced with what you have, but you've stuck it out, and we're all the better for it."

Her forehead crumpled again, and she spoke more quietly this time. "If your family doesn't understand you, if they always want you to be something else or to do something else, what makes you want to come back and fight for things the way you're doing now?"

*She can see parts of me no one's even acknowledged before.*

He took another step forward, and this time the soft warmth of her breath brushed his cheek as they stood only inches from each other. "Loyalty, I guess. No matter what anyone says or does in this family, there's a tectonic pull toward each other, and no matter how I try to make my own life, I guess my roots will always be here. Finding you here, being able to spend time with you, has certainly made me think my decision to come back was a good one."

Grace stared into Ari's face, and despite the reassuring tone of his voice, it was obvious that deep down he carried a whole lot of pain when it came to his family.

It broke her heart that he felt that way about his parents. There were obviously issues between Mano, Pia and their youngest son, and she wondered if it was because he was such a free spirit. He'd said to her more than once that he was only here out of a sense of duty, and did she really want to be with someone like that?

*Yes. Yes, you do.*

"I admire what you're doing," she said, her voice low. "Despite the fact you've felt like you were on the outside, you still stepped up and came when you were needed."

He stood a little straighter. "It was easier knowing you were here," he said, his dark eyes sparking.

"What do you mean?"

His lips tilted in a grin. "You understand my family's world and the world of weddings. I knew if I followed your lead, I couldn't go too far wrong."

Her cheeks heated as his gaze swept over her face. Why did he do this to her? Was it his confidence? The way he looked deep into her eyes when they were talking, as if she were the only woman in the world? The way he held himself, straight and strong? No, there was so much more to him than his beautiful body—and God knew she'd spent enough time appreciating that. Now she wanted to get to know who he was on the inside as well.

"It takes someone pretty special to fit in with my family," he said. "The intensity of the conversations, the constant drama of day-to-day life with the Katsalos family. But you have this amazing knack of making everyone feel special. That they've been listened to. I can't remember either my mother or my father saying a bad word about you, and take it from me, that's pretty unusual."

Her pulse tripped. He'd noticed that about her? She'd thought him so cool and detached whenever she'd been around him before. "Plenty of people wouldn't take the time to help out their family like you have," she said, wanting to know what really made him tick.

"You just do what you have to do when it comes to family, I guess. I've learned the best thing is not to have too many expectations of anyone. I used to hold them to some sort of high benchmark when it came to how they treated me and the way they treated each other, but the more I see human behavior in my work, the more I understand that people are flawed. We hurt each other, do bad things." He shrugged. "It's just the way we're made. Why should my family be any different?"

"Surely you don't think that about everyone? That everyone wants to, or is capable of hurting other people?" She smiled back at him, and her heart thudded harder in her chest. He didn't believe in a happily-ever-after?

Something deep within called to her to reach out to him, tell him he was wrong. She stepped closer.

"It's a mistake to rely on people, but sometimes you have a need for someone that just can't be satisfied without getting really close to them. As long as you understand that every one of us has flaws, then no one needs to end up hurt."

He picked up her hand, and her throat dried. "Grace," he said quietly. "I know you said that you didn't want things to move forward between us, but you've got to admit there's some pretty strong chemistry going on here, and I'm trying *really* hard to remember the reason why we shouldn't give in to it. Can you remind me what it was?"

She moistened her lips and tried to control her breathing. "We need to be focused in the next week," she heard herself say. "Thinking about everything that needs to be done."

"Thinking's overrated," he said as he stepped closer still and ran his knuckles down her cheek.

On reflex, she sucked in a breath as her skin burned. If she acted now, she'd avoid that point of no return—the moment when her body developed a will of its own and all rational thought disappeared for as long as she was with him.

As she looked up at him, her heart beating a million times a minute, it was clear the threshold had already been crossed.

"Instead of thinking, why don't we just go with the moment." He leaned in and brushed his lips lightly across hers, and sparks of heat ignited in her core. When he pulled back, he said with sincerity, "Of course, if at any point you were to tell me to stop, I'd do it."

She didn't want him to stop. Didn't want the tingling in her body to end, or the need to touch him to wane. Instinctively, she linked her hands behind his neck and pulled him in for another kiss.

His mouth was warm and sure, and his chest firm as he pressed closer. Her blood fizzed where he stroked her arm, and she lifted her face to deepen the kiss. The taste of him was everything she'd imagined—sweet and powerful. No stubble scratched her cheek. Instead, where she laid her palm against his face was warm and smooth.

She'd thought kissing him would feel forbidden and thrilling, but it was so much more. It ignited a different sort of fire within her—one where she was in control—where her response was strong. She opened her eyes, and he was watching her, watching her reactions to his touch, and it thrilled her even more.

"Grace," he moaned into her ear. "I've wanted this so long. Holding back when I thought you didn't want me was a killer."

She arched her neck, and he kissed a trail from her chin to the heated skin between her breasts. Her lungs were constricted, her heart speeding, and she'd die if he ever stopped.

When he lifted his face, he gently eased her back against the wall, and she let him guide her. For a long moment he didn't touch her, just looked deep into her eyes, and she thought she'd melt on the spot. When he did begin to move, it was to trail his fingers up both her arms, and she almost cried out with the perfection of his gentle touch. Every part of her skin was a mess of goose bumps, and she couldn't marshal a rational thought in her head.

Why was this a bad idea again? Why shouldn't she want a guy like Ari? All the reasons she'd been chanting to herself since the moment he'd sauntered back into her life were lost.

"Just fun," she murmured, to herself as much as to him. "I don't really do fun. The last time I did, I got hurt."

"Hurt?" he whispered as he kissed her behind her ear. "The last thing I would ever do is hurt you, Grace."

He kissed her again, and she squashed the warning bells that were ringing through her mind. She silenced them and kissed him deeper.

When he drew back, Ari pushed a strand of hair off her face. "You only have to say the word, and we can go right back to our old agreement."

"The agreement where we pretend not to want each other, and we commit to keeping our hands to ourselves twenty-four seven?" she breathed.

He chuckled as he rested his hands on her waist. "And take cold showers whenever we're around each other, and don't stop in our tracks when we hear the other's name? Yes, that agreement."

"I don't want anyone to know," she said haltingly. "I mean…we should be careful not to be seen by staff, and when your family gets here, I don't want any of the focus to be taken away from any of them."

"Why?" he asked as he moved his hands up her body.

"Well, for one thing," she said as she tried to focus, "I haven't dated since Mark…since my divorce. Except for that date with you, of course. And, since it's only a bit of fun, I don't want it to affect my reputation." The words seemed laughable, even to her own ears.

"I didn't realize you were the upholder of some squeaky-clean reputation." He chuckled in her ear.

"As a wedding planner," she said, "it's hard enough that I have one divorce under my belt. Having a string of broken relationships is not exactly good promo for my business."

"Okay," he said. "I get it. If you want to keep this strictly between you and me, that's fine. I'm used to secrets," he said as he stroked her shoulder. "And I've learned a few things over the years about how to fly under the radar. If that's what you really want, then that's the way it'll be."

Ari held Grace close as he reassured her. Of course, it made sense that she didn't want anyone to know about them, especially because he was probably not the sort of guy she'd imagined bringing home. But she'd obviously had a rough time in her marriage, and he could be patient until she felt more comfortable.

He remembered a warning his brother had given him a few months back about not getting involved with Grace, and it pricked his conscience for a second. Nick had said it could cause more problems for the Palace if things went wrong. But then he thought about how hard she'd kissed him back, and how she'd moaned quietly when he'd run his fingers up her bare arm. She wanted him as much as he did her, and that changed everything.

There was a noise at the door, and Grace jumped away from him. "Hey, Polly," she said breezily as her assistant came in.

"Sorry to interrupt," Polly said, "but I wondered if you'd be happy to see Congressman Williams. He's at the front desk."

"Oh, really!" Grace said, turning to Ari with a wooden

smile. "I wasn't expecting him. I thought it'd be Amy who'd come to organize everything."

"I'm more than happy to be there too," Ari said. "One of my family is bound to call and ask how things are going with the Williams wedding, so it makes sense for me to meet him as well."

"Okay," Polly said as she walked from the room. "I'll bring him through."

When Polly had left, Grace rounded her eyes at him. "That was a close enough call."

"I'm not going to leave you alone to talk to that guy," he said.

Grace shook her head. "I think it's best if you leave the congressman to me. I've had plenty of practice dealing with parents of the bride and groom. And you know how important it is that every aspect of this wedding goes smoothly."

Ari leaned against her desk. "Let's just say I know this guy's reputation, and I don't want you dealing with him on your own."

Grace's mouth set in a line. "You're not just saying that because there's something going on between us now?"

He frowned, puzzled by how quickly she'd run hot and cold. "What do you mean?"

"If you didn't feel you had some sort of claim on me, would you still be here to protect me?"

"Claim?" Had he heard her right?

Her voice softened, as if she was measuring what she said. "If I were just another woman who worked for you, would you have to stay here while I did my job, or would you be happy to let me talk to a man who wanted to do business with me?"

"Grace," Ari said, dropping his voice. "I'm not going to let a man who's being investigated for sexual harassment be near any woman. And especially not you right here."

"You know that for a fact about him, do you?" she said, clearly testing him.

He shrugged. "There's been some talk. Some innuendo."

"And if I asked you to leave and let me deal with this myself?"

Why would she ask that of him? Why would she not let him support her? Something made him realize this wasn't about him, but about someone in her past, and he wanted to let her know it would be okay.

He pushed himself off the desk, and when he was beside her, took her hand. "While you're with me you will feel protected and cared for. That doesn't make you weak, and it doesn't mean I don't have the utmost respect for you. This is not about me thinking you're a fragile woman; it's because I protect the people I care about. While this is on my watch, I'll be here for you."

"I don't need protecting, Ari. I don't need a man to tell me what is and isn't good for me."

Stung, he stepped back. "Grace, I'm sorry."

She dropped her chin, and he could've kicked himself. There was a whole lot more going on here than a woman who wanted to do her job, and his chest tightened at the pain she was projecting.

Before he could say any more, Polly ushered the congressman in. "Katsalos," the man said, shaking his hand firmly. "I believe I dealt with your brother when we first discussed my daughter's wedding, so I assume I don't need to run over all the details again."

"Yes, you would've talked to my brother Nick, but the person you'll need to deal with from this point on is Grace Bennett. She's the best in her field."

The congressman acknowledged Grace, but then he turned right back to Ari. "Right, there's an awful lot to be done, and not a lot of time to be doing it. I'm prepared to spend whatever it takes to make this everything my daughter wants, and because I'm paying you, now that stupid wager hasn't worked out, I expect everything to be kept completely confidential."

"Confidential?" Grace said.

"Yes, my daughter and her fiancé aren't thrilled the wedding is happening earlier than we'd originally planned, but circumstances make it a necessity. I don't want that communicated to anyone at all, do you understand?"

"Of course," Grace said as she offered the congressman a chair. "You have our confidence, and be assured that Amy will have the wedding of her dreams."

As the congressman rattled off a list of all the plans he expected the Palace to fulfill for his daughter, Grace looked past him to Ari. The smallest tilt in her lips and the warmth in her eyes told him he'd done the right thing by staying here with her. It was clear Grace carried a heavy burden deep within, and he vowed to help her with it in any way he could.

"Time we called it a day?" Ari said after the congressman had left.

Grace glanced at the clock. "More like night. I didn't realize it was so late." She smiled at him, relieved they now had a plan for the Williams wedding and a way forward for a busy week. "Thanks so much for staying."

He took a step toward her and hooked his arm around her waist. "Couldn't think of anywhere I'd rather be," he said and kissed her.

There was a knock on the office door, and his hand dropped away. Grace turned to see the door open, and Polly put her head around. "I'm off now—got a Zumba class with my name on it, unfortunately—but I thought you might like to come and take a look at Monty. He's not looking too good."

"What's up?" Ari asked as he straightened his collar. His lips were still damp from where she'd kissed him. When they were alone again, she intended carrying on right where they'd left off.

"Nothing I can put my finger on," Polly said over her shoulder as they followed her out the door. "He's just not his normal cranky and obnoxious self."

They followed Polly across the courtyard and over to Monty's cage. When they got there, the parrot was on the ground surrounded by feathers, and the way he was burrowing his beak into his back, it looked like he was trying to rip out more. "Think I should call the vet?" Polly asked.

Grace rubbed her hand across her chin. "No, you go to your class, Polly. I'll take care of this."

"Have you seen him like this before?" Grace asked when Polly had left.

"I don't remember," Ari said as he moved around to the door of the aviary. "He's Dad's pride and joy, so he's always been the one to take care of him." He opened the door, stepped in, and closed it behind him. "Who's been taking care of him while Mom and Dad have been away?"

Grace put her hands on her hips. "I guess we've just shared it. Pavlo took over the feeding—he always seemed to be out here with a spare cabbage or corn cob—and one of the gardeners has been cleaning his cage, I think. Your dad asked Polly to keep an eye on Monty and Boris, the cat we've been looking after for Mara, your cousin's girlfriend." Monty burrowed his beak into his chest and seemed to be scratching hard. "Maybe it's separation anxiety. He could be missing Mano."

Ari made soft sounds and moved closer with his arms held out. "See, he'd normally fly up and land on my arm when I was this close, but he's pretty miserable." He shrugged out of his denim jacket then crouched close to the bird. "*Ela re,*" he said softly, his arm held out to the parrot. "*Ela tho.*"

The bird just blinked at him, a stray piece of down stuck to his beak. "Dad used to sit for hours out here talking to Monty in Greek," Ari said in a quiet voice. "I thought it was kind of crazy at the time, but they seemed to love each other's company." He got closer, but the parrot didn't move, and he carefully covered Monty's body with his jacket then picked him up.

"Oh, he looks so sad," Grace said as she clutched one of the bars. The sight of big, tough Ari holding the bird so gently almost brought tears to her eyes. After all that had transpired, she couldn't imagine telling Mano something had happened to his special bird. "I hope he's going to be okay."

"I think there's a vet over on Baker Street; I'll take him there," Ari said. "Although I don't think he'd appreciate a lift on my bike." He joined her on the other side of the bars, and when he moved closer, she stroked Monty's beak. The bird's eyes were closed, and he was making a snuffling noise.

She looked up at Ari. "It's times like this I feel like a complete idiot for not having a car."

"It's okay," he said as he tucked Monty under his arm. "I'll get an Uber."

"I'm coming with you," she said, pulling out her phone. "I think there's a carry cage in the back office. Why don't you get it, and I'll get him ready?"

Half an hour later, they were sitting in the air-conditioned waiting room of the vet's office. The vet had taken Monty away for tests and said she hoped to have results within the hour if they'd like to wait.

Ari crossed his ankles and leaned back in the seat. Bits of down and feather still stuck to his T-shirt where he'd held

Monty close. "One of the hardest things about living in the city is not being able to have a pet."

Grace pushed away a pile of old magazines and moved closer to him on the orange vinyl couch. "You couldn't have a cat?"

He looked over at her and grinned. "I look like a cat lover?"

"Maybe," she said. "I could picture you with a gnarly old tom cat. A black one with scars from all his street fights."

He reached down and threaded his fingers through hers. "A rough old tom cat, you think?"

"Or a big old marmalade girl who wouldn't take any nonsense from anyone."

"And if I chose a dog instead?"

She squeezed his hand. "A bitzer."

"What sort of breed is that?"

"Bits of everything." She laughed. "I'd say your match in the dog world would be a big old mix of everything. Maybe the body of a Ridgeback, the temperament of a Saint Bernard, and the energy of a Border collie."

"I like it," he said, nodding. "Although it doesn't sound like he'd be the most handsome dog on the block."

She looked at him sideways and grinned. "Oh, he'd be handsome, all right. All the lady dogs would be lining up to be seen out on the town with him."

She turned to face him. "So, what about me? Cat or dog?"

"Easy," he said with a teasing grin. "Pedigree cat."

"What kind?"

"Hmmm," he said, eyes narrowed. "What are those ones with the really superior look on their faces? The fluffy ones."

"Superior?" she said, and playfully thumped his arm.

"No, not a cat," he said. "You'd be a greyhound. A sleek, beautiful greyhound who works all day and all night and lies around looking like a princess."

She leaned into him, and he pulled her closer. "Ever owned a dog?"

"Yeah." Her throat constricted.

"Tell me about him." When he saw the look on her face, he became more serious.

"Reggie. A black miniature schnauzer." She hadn't said his name in so long, she had to take a deeper breath to carry on. "When I left Mark, it was kinda in a hurry, and I stayed with my friend Meg. Her apartment building didn't allow dogs, and when it came to Mark and I dividing our things up, he felt that Reg had been away from me too long."

He stroked her hair. "Still miss him, huh?"

She laughed lightly. "Every time I open a packet of chips, I expect to see him racing around the corner."

"You'll have a dog again, and a car, and a great new business." He kissed her on the forehead. "You're going places, Grace Bennett. I can tell."

She breathed in the warm cotton scent of his T-shirt. "I don't know what I'll do if something's really wrong with Monty," she said. "If I'd been paying more attention, not letting things get so on top of me, maybe I'd have noticed sooner he wasn't well."

"Hey, he'll be fine," Ari said. "He's survived cupcakes and pieces of confetti and discarded party poppers, and once he ate the icing off the top of a wedding cake. I'm sure he's going to be fine."

"It's funny," Grace said as she relaxed into him, the stress of the day and the week to come melting away while they sat there together. "I've been a part of the Palace for so long, and yet it's only now I really feel I know it."

"You mean you're starting to see it warts and all?"

"Yeah, something like that. You give everything such a raw honesty. Nothing's hidden with you, and I like that."

He lifted her chin and kissed her. "Funny, you've given me a whole new perspective on the place as well."

Footsteps came toward them from down a corridor, and a nurse in a purple smock appeared holding Monty. "Nothing more than a common bacterial infection," she said. "We've given him some antibiotics, and he should be fine in a day or two."

"And his bald patches?" Grace asked.

"They'll grow back. He's in pretty good condition for an old guy."

"That's such a relief," Grace said as she opened the door to the cage and the nurse put him in.

"No way I'd want to tell Dad we'd lost his pride and joy," Ari said with a smile.

"Now all we have to do is make sure we manage his other pride and joy," Grace said as she closed the door to the cage and handed it to Ari. "Two weeks, four weddings, and the whole of the Katsalos family back here. I'd say we need to buckle in. It could be a bumpy flight."

5

---

*L*ate the next morning, Grace passed her laptop to Ari. After the visit to the vet's last night, Monty seemed to be doing fine, and it'd been a good feeling coming in to help again today. Boris, the cat they were looking after while his cousin Alex and his girlfriend were traveling, was curled up on a cushion by the window, and Ari couldn't help feeling a bit of the cat's contentment right now. He was going to enjoy getting to know Grace a whole lot better.

"So, the list marked on here is all the things we need to have done before Nick and Erin get here on Thursday," she explained, dragging her hand across her brow. "And then the second list is what I'd like us to have finished by the time your mom gets back. It'd be good to know exactly when your dad will be here as well."

"I'll try to get in touch with him," Ari said, staring at the screen. "You're going to have to tell me what all this stuff is, remember? Words and I don't mix."

She smiled, pulled a piece of paper toward her on the desk and methodically checked things off. "I've highlighted the list, and if you just push that play button at the top of the screen, it'll read everything back to you."

"Sorry?" He looked back at the screen. There was the triangular button she was talking about.

"I've added an extension so the computer can read the list back to you," she said as she wrote something on the paper.

He pushed the laptop back to her. He'd been dealing with his reading issues for long enough to know there was no point trying, but the sense of failure always stung. "I promise it'll turn out better if you just tell me what needs to be done."

She lifted her chin and grinned, but pushed the computer back. "Haven't you used text to speech on a computer before? It's like Siri on an iPhone. Here, I'll show you."

She came and stood beside him. Her usual scent of flowers and sunshine enveloped him, and the memory of her lips on his as they'd said goodbye last night powered through his blood. She'd asked him in for a drink, and he'd had to round up all his willpower to say no. She'd looked really tired, and the early night had clearly done her good. But as she leaned closer, he had to will himself to concentrate on the screen.

"Don't own an iPhone," he said, as she hovered the cursor over the play button. "I just use my phone to make calls. Novel, right? Even predictive text has no idea what I'm trying to spell in a message. I'm my own text fail meme."

"It's just like an audio book," she said, ignoring his attempt at deflection. "You use those, right?" There wasn't judgment or concern in her baby blues, just a whole lot of caring.

He crossed his arms. "You think I'm someone who listens to Shakespeare while I'm burning up Highway One?"

"Oh, I thought I saw a book cover on your phone when I was at your place. Anyway, it doesn't matter. Just listen to this."

She pushed the triangle, and a woman's voice read the words back to them.

"You can have a guy reading it if you like," she said as she played with the computer settings. "Look, he can even have a Scottish accent." She pushed the button again, and a rich Scottish brogue read out the list of jobs to be done, making them both laugh at the sound. The list had sounded pretty mundane before, but the way the dude said it made it seem kinda interesting. She pushed a slider to the right and the voice doubled in speed.

She laughed again as she turned to him, and his heart squeezed tight.

"I can't believe no one's ever shown you this before," she said.

He shrugged. "I quit school before I should've, and I guess I've just avoided anything too technical. Not being able to decipher an instruction manual and all that."

"Then you don't need to do that anymore," she said firmly. "That's what iPads and computers are for—to help people do things they can't do on their own."

He was silent for a minute, and she looked back at him. "You're really no different from me. I can't add a row of numbers to save myself. If I didn't have a spreadsheet with all its auto formulas, I'd be in a constant state of panic."

"So, does that mean I'm not so special after all?" he asked. "I've always had this vision of myself being different to everyone else. That I had a secret part of me I could never tell anyone about." He threw her a smile. "I'm not sure how I feel about being the same as everyone else."

"Trust me," she said with a sexy grin. "You're definitely not the same as everyone else." He chuckled as he pushed the triangle and the Scottish dude read the list right through. Boris lifted his head from the cushion and looked at him disdainfully, and when it ended, Grace looked up from her own list. "Maybe if we work backward from Erin and Nick's wedding, we can make sure we have all the bases covered. I was thinking that if it's at all possible, we should have the rehearsal dinner here. I was wondering about asking Leo if he could cook, just for that one night."

"Why here?" he asked. "I could book a restaurant."

"Well, it'll have been a long time since your dad and Patterson have had anything to do with each other, and I figured it'd be nice for your dad to be entertaining on his territory."

Ari nodded. "Good thinking. Mom and Dad haven't seen all the renovations Nick and Yasmin have done either, so it makes even more sense to have it here."

Grace started moving each of her fingers.

"What are you doing?"

"Counting," she said with a laugh. "I can never add up in my head properly. The spreadsheet thing, remember? I think we should count on eleven people. That is, unless Erin's sisters have partners."

"I don't get eleven," he said, staring at her graceful hand and the pink polish that was the same blush as her cheeks. "I get twelve."

"Mr. and Mrs. Patterson, Erin's two sisters, Nick and Erin, Yasmin and Lane, your parents and you," she said with a smile.

"You'll be there too," he said.

She blinked. "We're keeping things between us quiet, remember?"

He touched her hand and linked his fingers through hers. "But you're an enormous part of the wedding, and I want you there."

She chewed her lip. "We'd have to be careful no one suspects anything is going on."

He shrugged. "I don't see why it's such a big deal if they find out, but if that's what you want."

"It is what I want," she said. "But it'd be nice to be part of the evening, and maybe I can help smooth things between your dad and Patterson."

"Good luck with that," he said, scrolling through the list. "What's your main priority for the week?"

"Well, Erin and Nick get back on Thursday. I said I'd meet Erin at her parents' place at four to go over the plans."

"I'll come too," he said. "I'd like to speak to Nick about my mom and dad and what he thinks we can do to make being back here a good experience for them."

"That's so sweet," she said. "See, you really do believe in love and marriage."

"I never said I didn't believe in love," he said. "It's the tragedy of marriage that really gets to me. My parents have been married for more than forty years, and neither of them are happy."

"I know," she said quietly.

"In my heart, I think they'd be better off going their separate ways." He blew out a breath. "But they've changed each other so much, I don't know if they could function on their own anymore."

It sucked to say that, but he'd been thinking about it for a while. Why stay in a marriage where two people were miserable, or even one for that matter, instead of cutting your losses and having a shot at happiness?

Grace sighed and shook her head. "Maybe this wedding will help bring them back together." She looked at her watch. "You know, it's past six o'clock. I've been working you hard all afternoon. Perhaps we should call it a night."

"Why don't I come back to your place for a while?" Ari said. "We can do some more planning for next week. We could get takeout."

~

"What? You're not going to offer to cook me dinner?" Grace asked, turning to the window. In the distance, Monty squawked loudly. He'd been so much better with the antibiotics the vet had given him and sounded even more excited than usual.

"It's okay. He'll be telling Boris cat to keep his distance," Ari said, obviously sensing her distraction. "Trust me, you don't want me near a kitchen," he said. "My mom was such a good cook that none of us were ever allowed in the kitchen. Nick and Yasmin are bad enough at cooking, but I've got no clue."

"Maybe I'm going to have to teach you," she said with a grin.

A loud noise came from the entranceway, and Ari leaped out of his seat. "Are you expecting anyone?" he asked, his body taut as if ready to pounce.

"No, I locked up after Polly left. There shouldn't be anyone else here until morning." She stood up, but he waved her to sit back down.

"Wait here while I check it out," he said, voice low.

He slowly opened the office door, and when he'd moved through into the restaurant, she followed him, her heart hammering.

She stopped and watched through the gap in the door. He made his way around the perimeter of the room like a wildcat stalking its prey, his gaze fixed on the door at the other end. His police training was obvious, and it made her feel protected, something she hadn't felt in a long time.

The handle on the outside door rattled, and Ari reached down to his ankle. She covered her mouth with her hand. He had a gun?

From behind the door there was a commotion followed

by someone cursing loudly, and to her enormous relief, she realized it was Mano.

Ari must've realized, too, as his body relaxed. Straightening the bottom of his jeans, he walked over to the door, flicked the lock, and turned the handle.

She was about to leave the office and welcome back her boss, but something stopped her. Mano was exclaiming loudly in Greek and had his son in a tight bear hug. Ari, in turn, had his father's head cradled in his hand and was replying in Greek. Ari was taller than his dad, and when he placed a kiss on top of the older man's head, tears pooled in her eyes.

Mano stepped back, and with both hands on his son's shoulders, looked into his face and shook him. Ari laughed, and Grace wished she knew what was passing between them.

But it was the love on their faces that made breath stall in her lungs. This wasn't a son who was marginalized by his family, and this wasn't a father who was disappointed in his son. The love that had enveloped this room when Ari and Mano saw each other again was palpable.

She could've watched the two of them all day, but she suddenly realized another, much younger man, dressed in an expensive looking jacket and jeans, stood beside Mano. Ari must have just noticed him, too, as he strode towards him and enveloped him in a bear hug.

All three proceeded to speak loudly in Greek, slapping each other on the back then gesturing wildly with their arms. Eventually, Ari nodded toward his father's bags, but Mano said something and they both looked towards her.

Heat spread across her cheeks as she realized how it must look, her standing there watching them, but her embarrassment was lost as Mano exclaimed, "Grace!" and hurried over.

"It is very good to see you again, *koukla*. I have been so worried about you having all the responsibility for things here, but now I am back, and you don't need to worry anymore. Not at all. Nicky told me not to come back and get in the way of all your work, but I had to see things here for myself. I hope you understand."

He stepped closer and kissed her on both cheeks. He smelled of warm wool and Wild Moss aftershave. "Of course, after so long away, I have forgotten my keys, and it was lucky that Ari was here to let me and Costa in, or we might have given you a big fright."

"Grace, this is my cousin Costa," Ari said, and Costa came forward and shook her hand. "Costa usually lives in Switzerland, but he helped Dad get back quickly and he'll stay for Nick and Erin's wedding."

"Costa has his own plane," Mano said as he slapped his nephew on the back. "Who'd have thought a boy from the village would be so successful. My brother always was the smart one and he certainly has a smart son."

"Nice to meet you, Grace," Costa said in polished English with a rich accent.

"Oh, we have met before," Grace said, remembering when both Yasmin and Nick used to call their parents in Greece. "Mano was staying with your father, and I talked to you on FaceTime a few times."

"Ah, that's right," Costa said. "My dad and uncle are not so good with technology so it was lucky I was there to help them learn. They're both pretty good at using it now."

"Would you like to come in for coffee or…?"

"Please excuse me," Costa said, "but I need to head back to the city for the night. Everything okay, *Theio*?"

"Yes, yes," Mano said as he slapped Costa on the shoulder again. "I can't thank you enough Costaki."

"Yes, thanks, Costa," Ari said as he followed his cousin to the door. "Will we see you at the rehearsal dinner?"

"I'd love to be there," his cousin said.

When Costa had gone, Grace looked back at Mano. His face was more lined than when he'd left for Greece, his hair grayer, but his always expressive deep-brown eyes sparkled. "It's so good to see you, Mano. How are you?" she asked.

Mano shook his head and placed his carry bag on the ground. His normally loud voice became softer. "I am not good, Grace," he said sadly. "After all these months, I have not managed to win back my Pia. We have spoken so many times, but she still refuses to come home with me until I agree to many changes with the Palace and the way we live our lives."

Grace looked past Mano to his son, and Ari gave a one-shouldered shrug.

"I'm so sorry," Grace said as she rubbed his back. "I'd been hoping you two would have had some quiet time to talk things through."

"Quiet! Bah," Mano exclaimed. "On Lesvos, there are always people around and there is always work to be done. Nothing is ever quiet with Pia's sister there all the time like a thirsty goat. I live with my own brother and yet Pia's sister always seems to find me when I'm drinking coffee in the *plateia*. You'd think it would be busier here with a business to run, but it's not. It feels like I have to come back here for a holiday."

"Maybe when Pia comes back for Nick's wedding there will be time for the two of you to talk," Grace said hopefully.

"And then there's Yasmin and Lane's wedding," Ari added, "and after that there's bound to be some grandchildren arriving. That's got to make Mom want to—"

"I don't *want* her to come back here just because of Nicky or any grandchildren!" Mano said forcefully. "I want her to come back because she loves *me* and can't imagine spending her life anywhere else or *with* anyone else. Aristotle, I know you think I am old and foolish, but I love your mother so much it hurts me here," he said, thumping his chest. His voice cracked. "And I will fight for her until she realizes that she loves me *too*."

The power and passion with which Mano spoke brought tears to Grace's eyes. Of course, she'd always guessed he loved his wife, but he was a man who liked to do things properly and wouldn't give much of himself away in front of employees. He'd been such a hard worker as well, and it was heartbreaking to think they still weren't together.

"Okay, Pop," Ari said as he moved forward, breaking the tension. "You'll be tired after your trip." He patted his father's shoulder. "Why don't I take your bags up to the house, and we can catch up properly tomorrow."

"I should leave the house to Pia," Mano said, his face downcast.

"She won't be coming tonight," Ari said as he picked up Mano's bag. "You can stay tonight, and then we'll sort something else out in the morning."

His father nodded and turned to Grace. "Good night, *koukla mou*, I will see you in the morning. There is much to be done in the next week, and I want to be at my best."

"Good night," Grace said as she watched both men leave. After working here for so long, she'd felt she knew everything about everyone, but seeing Mano's heartbreak now, and watching the way Ari had so gently related to his father, had her questioning the way she'd been so ready to judge him. It made her want to do her very best for this family.

Half an hour later, a soft knock sounded at her apartment door. After she'd said good night to Mano and Ari, she'd double-checked that all the outside gates to the Palace were locked, so it had to be Ari.

"It's me," he said, in confirmation. "I didn't want to leave without saying goodbye."

She raced to the tiny mirror above the hall table and raked her fingers through her hair. God, she was a mess. She straightened her blouse, yanked her skirt straight, and took a deep breath. When she unlocked the door to her apartment, Ari was standing there like some kind of priceless Greek statue, one hand on her doorframe.

Her pulse fluttered in her throat. Did she have any beer in the house? Any coffee? Had she put on her comfy beige bra this morning, or the red one with the little bow?

"Hey," he said. "Sorry if I disturbed you."

"No, no," she said. "I was…well to be honest, I was making myself grilled cheese. Do you want some?"

His mouth tilted in a grin. "Grilled cheese sounds awesome."

She stood back and waved him in. "How's your dad? Is he okay?"

"He's okay, I guess. He's not going to find it easy to take a backseat while he's here, but I'd like him to. He seems really tired, you know?" He stopped, his hands in his pockets. "Wow, you've done a lot to this place." He looked around. "My grandparents used to stay here when they visited from Greece, and it was nothing like this then. My mom used to keep plastic over the furniture so that everything would stay really nice."

The walls she'd painted a soft green, and the cute rug she'd got on sale—this place was really a part of her now. It was going to be a wrench when she had to move out. In more ways than one.

"I don't go out a lot," she said over her shoulder as she moved into the kitchen and he followed. "Work takes up most of my time, and I don't like to have friends over when your parents are around, so I've spent a bit of time decorating."

He picked up her yearly horoscope book, which had been sitting on the table, and thumbed the pages. "So, this is where you found out that Scorpios and Libras weren't a good match?" He tipped a grin. "You really believe this stuff?"

"Yeah, I do," she said. "My grandma always seemed to understand people. She was such a good judge of character, and when I asked her about it one day, she said it was because she'd worked out their star sign. Of course, some of it's hokey, but the more you read, the more it kinda fits." She opened the refrigerator door. "I don't have any beer, sorry. Wine?"

"Sure."

She busied herself getting the wine and grilled cheese as he flicked through the book. He was quiet for a while then said, "Hey, listen to this. 'The Scorpio man has the need to always speak his mind, and in general, he will speak the truth. It could be said that his biggest joy lies in giving his observations of the hard truth that nobody wants to deal with.' I reckon that sounds exactly like me, don't you?"

She came back into the room and put a wine bottle and two glasses on the table then sat on the couch with her feet tucked up. "What sort of hard truths would they be?"

He tapped the book on the table. "What we were talking about before. About marriage and how it makes people unhappy. That if people could accept other people's faults and not try to change them, things might work out better."

He really believed what he'd said about marriage? Where did that come from? Was it just through his work, or had he been burned by a relationship in the past?

"Let's see what it says about Libras in relationships," he said.

She poured the wine, and Ari read again. "It can be hard

to understand her position because she'll rarely show her uncontrolled emotions and passions, so the right partner needs to know her deeply and intimately, including the things she doesn't want to show." His eyes sparkled. "Sound like you?"

She shrugged. "Maybe. I like to think I don't keep my feelings too covered up, but maybe that's true."

"What star sign was your husband?" he asked, his attention still focused on the pages of the book.

Grace's heart stalled, and her throat wouldn't move to swallow the wine. When she didn't answer, Ari's chin lifted, and his face changed. "Hey, I'm sorry. I didn't mean to—"

"It's fine," she said, then took another sip of the wine to compose herself. "It's been a long time since anyone's mentioned him, that's all."

Ari's gaze intensified. "I'm sorry if I upset you."

He came and sat down beside her, and the scent of him— his raw, male presence—made her more conflicted about telling him this. It was precisely those physical things that she'd let rule her feelings for Mark, and here she was doing it all over again.

"We didn't end on very good terms, and thinking about it makes me angry and sad," she said as she twirled the glass in her hands. "I'd wanted to leave for a long time before I actually did, and I've pushed away a lot of those memories."

He turned to face her, his dark, expressive gaze roaming her face. "Where did you live when you were married?"

It made sense that he'd ask lots of questions; he was an investigator after all. But he didn't need to know the whole truth. "Not far from here," she said, thinking about the beautiful house she'd had, the pretty cottage garden she'd spent hours creating. The rules and the threats.

"Oh, I'd imagined you'd lived in the city," he said. "When

you said you didn't have a car, I guessed it was because you didn't need one."

She took another mouthful, and this time the wine burned the back of her throat. "It's not that I didn't need one."

Should she tell him anything more? This was only a bit of fun, no attachments, no expectations. She didn't need to know all about him, and he didn't need to know all about her. Especially not that stuff.

"So, you didn't like the responsibility of driving?" he asked, misreading what she'd said. "Yasmin was a bit like that when she was younger, but now that she's cheated death, she's fearless. Apparently, she and Lane have been canyoning in Italy. I kind of feel you're fearless too."

She looked down at her hands then back up at him. "I'm not fearless at all."

She'd lost so much confidence in herself, living with Mark, that she hadn't even trusted herself behind the wheel. Fearful, maybe. Fearless, no.

"But you've taken a chance on me," he said, leaning further into the seat—making himself at home. "Maybe I'm your first step toward throwing caution to the wind. Maybe in a few weeks you'll let me help you find a car that really suits you."

He did make her feel safe, but that was the problem. She'd gotten it so wrong in the past when she'd been attracted to someone with charisma and a strong sense of their own sexuality. Look how it had ended with Mark.

Grace smiled at him. "You're different than I'd imagined."

He sat closer to her on the couch and touched her hand. Warmth surged into her chest, and she shivered when his rough hands skimmed across her skin. His voice dropped low, like aged whiskey, smooth and possibly lethal. And his gaze pinned her to the spot. "How had you imagined me?"

"Kind of arrogant, I guess. You know, when someone is as good-looking as you are, it's kind of off-putting. I remember when we had a wedding here once, and you arrived on your motorcycle. None of the female guests could keep their eyes off you."

*Including me.*

He laughed out loud. "And here was me thinking you didn't consider me enough for you. When I tried to kiss you on that date, I could've sworn you were backing away. I wondered if you rubbed off the taste of me with the back of your hand when you got inside."

"It wasn't like that," she said, and dropped her gaze, the rush to be close to him scrambling her brain. "It was almost like…you're too beautiful."

He brushed a strand of hair from her face, and she couldn't fight the shiver as she looked up. "You're the beautiful one," he murmured. "I remember the very first time I met you here. I was supposed to be coming home for Easter, but I'd been called out to a big job, and Mom was telling me how disappointed she was in me. And then you walked in with your hair all loose around your face. You were wearing a floaty white top and took my breath away."

She touched his arm, and the strong muscles tensed beneath his navy blue shirt. Every part of him was taut, as if ready to spring, and it made her giddy with desire for him. She leaned in and placed her lips on his, and he kissed her back. He ran his tongue along her bottom lip, and when he found the inside of her mouth, she moaned. His hands cupped her shoulders, and he drew her closer so that her weight was resting against him.

"I've always noticed you," he whispered, when he'd ended the kiss. "The way you light up a room with your smile. The way you make people feel comfortable whatever the situation. When you stepped back from me on that first date, it was like a stab in my gut."

"It wasn't you," she whispered. "I'm sorry. I can't ever imagine you making me feel bad."

As her heart rate spiked and a warm sweat inched its way up her body, she pulled back. Her head was spinning, her mouth dry—all signs that soon she would lose her head and be at the mercy of her instincts and Ari's touch.

As if sensing her hesitation, he slowed the kisses against her skin. "It's only me," he whispered. "We can take this as slowly or as swiftly as you like, you only have to say the word."

"And if I wanted you to stop?" she asked breathlessly.

"If you wanted me to stop, then I would hold you close until that thought passed and I could touch you again," he said. "It's you and me alone in this, Grace." He reached down and squeezed her hand. "I'm willing to wait until you're ready. Until you can really relax and be with me in the moment."

She'd never been spoken to like this by a man. Given permission—no, encouraged—to take the lead, to decide how she wanted this to work. Do and feel as she wanted. The trust he had in her, the belief and caring, was the biggest turn-on of them all.

Like a drowning woman, she reached for him and held him close. Tight. She pressed her lips against his again, but this time willing their bodies to be joined, and when he kissed her back, she groaned with the heady thrill of it.

Desperate to get closer, she pushed up his shirt until she met the warm firmness of his stomach, which trembled as she slid her fingers across the smooth muscle. And it was everything she'd imagined. Touching his flesh, getting close to the blood that ran in his veins to the heart she was now a part of. As he kissed her ear, his intake of breath was swift, and it was clear he wanted her just as much as she wanted him.

He pulled back and held her gaze. "I want you to want this as much as I do," he said as his eyes sparked.

"You can't know how many times I've imagined your hands on my skin," she gasped. "Your fingers exploring every piece of me." She raised her arms above her head, inviting him to take her blouse off—to get as close as he possibly could.

As he lifted the blouse over her head, she pushed every negative thought from her mind. He made her feel safe. He made her feel wanted and desired, and that was the greatest turn-on she'd had in years. With her blouse a puddle on the floor, he gently put both his hands at her waist, and a surge of goose bumps swept across her skin. Beneath her bra, her nipples contracted into painful peaks that yearned for his most intimate touch. Slowly, agonizingly, he trailed his fingertips up her torso, all the while keeping his gaze fixed firmly on hers.

When he reached her breasts, he let his fingers skim lightly over the fabric of her bra and then cupped his hands on her shoulders. It was as if she were in a trance, immobile with the power of his stare and the warmth radiating from his touch to her very core.

"Kiss me," she whispered. "You make me feel alive again, and I want to know that this is all real."

He leaned closer until his breath warmed her cheek. "Are you sure?" He turned his hands over so his nails were resting on her skin, then he dragged them, ever so softly, down the tops of her arms to her elbows.

"I'm ready," she moaned. "I've never been more ready in my life."

6

The next evening, as she got ready for dinner, Grace
glanced in the mirror for the sixteenth time. Pink
blouse, navy skirt, and wedges. Was her outfit formal
enough? Casual enough? Did she look like the wedding planner, or someone who was meeting her lover's family for the
first time? The whole of the Katsalos family would be there
tonight, as well as some of Erin's family—it was kind of a
rehearsal of the rehearsal dinner—a chance for the two families to meet each other before the wedding.

*And where do I fit in?*

She shook her head. Of course, only she and Ari knew
they were lovers. And the reminder of that was her eyes,
gritty from a lack of sleep last night, and the warm, languid
caress in her body whenever she thought of herself wrapped
in Ari's arms. Polly had arranged everything for the dinner
tonight while Grace was at Patterson's. When she'd got back,
she'd initially said no when Ari had insisted she join them for
dinner. But he was persuasive. She would be a good mediator
between Mr. Patterson and Mano, and she could answer any
questions anyone had about the big day.

She laid a hand on her chest and tried to still her breathing. Ari had said he'd come early and bring her downstairs tonight for the dinner, but she wondered if that would be a giveaway. Whenever she was around him, her skin burned. Maybe people knew she couldn't tear her gaze away from him. No, she reassured herself. This night was about Erin and Nick. No one would even notice that she came in with Ari.

When there was a soft knock, she collected her evening bag and opened the door. Ari stood in front of her in a perfectly cut, navy blue suit with a cream shirt that made his eyes even more deeply caramel. His skin shone bronze in the light from her hallway, and his teeth when he smiled were bright white.

He stepped forward and drew her to him. She breathed deep his clean, freshly showered scent, and immediately her rushing heartbeat skipped lighter. "You look incredible," he whispered in her ear. "Thank you for being with me tonight."

The way he spoke to her, as if she were the most precious thing in the world, made her want to melt into a pool at his feet. "You're perfectly hot yourself," she said as she stroked the cool cotton of his collar.

"The others haven't arrived yet. I knew you wouldn't want to make an entrance with me, so I thought we could greet everyone as they came in."

He leaned back when she adjusted her blouse and scanned her face. "Grace Bennett, are you nervous?"

She dropped her chin. "Of course, I'm nervous. In these next few days, I need to pull off two hugely important weddings, I get to see your whole family again, and I have to pretend you and I aren't together."

He stroked a finger down her cheek, and her whole body came alight. "I'm here to help you with those first two things, every step of the way. And you know I'd be just as happy if my family knew we were seeing each other. It's lucky Mom insisted you be part of the dinner before I had to make some excuse."

She blew out a breath. "Ari, have you ever had the feeling you were reborn? That the world suddenly looked completely different?"

His forehead wrinkled, but his mouth turned up in a smile. "Maybe. When I finally made it into the police force after I thought I'd never qualify. That felt pretty good."

"It's like that for me," she said, taking his hands in hers. "When I was finally on my own again after my marriage finished, it felt like I was born again, like my slate was clean. And that's made me want to do things right this time. Not make mistakes, not settle for second best. I need us to keep this quiet until we're both sure what it is that we have."

Ari nuzzled her neck, and she leaned into him. "I think I know what we have here. Something pretty damn good."

He placed a kiss at the corner of her mouth. "Have you ever heard my sister's mindfulness bell?"

"Yes!" she said. "It used to go off all the time when she was back working here with Lane, and your uncle Leo could never get used to it. One time he thought it was an oven timer and ruined a prize soufflé."

"That's what I think you and I need," he said. "A bell that reminds us to stay in the here and now, not compare anything we have now to our past, or try to imagine what sort of future there might be for us."

"Okay, point taken." Grace reached up to press her lips against his. "I'm enjoying what we have right now."

"This is a pretty significant day for my family," Ari said. "The first time we're all back at the Palace. The first time Mom and Dad have been back together."

"And I'm honored to be sharing it with you. I'm going to miss them when I'm gone." She meant that. Bone deep. The

Katsalos family had not only helped her through the toughest time in her life, they'd also helped her believe in herself again —not only Ari, but all of them. Ironically, it was their love and support that had helped her make this leap to be with someone like Ari.

"How is your mom?" Pia had arrived yesterday, but Grace had been so busy over at Patterson's, she hadn't had a chance to catch up with her boss yet.

"She's great. Happier than I've seen her in years, and surprisingly relaxed given that she's about to be the mother of the bridegroom. I can see she loves Erin, so that's made things easier, I guess."

"It'd be pretty awful if a mom didn't like the partner of one of her children."

Ari grinned. "We all know how much she loves you already, so that's not gonna be an issue." He reached for her hand. "Ready?"

Grace's knees went weak at the loving look he gave her. How had she gotten so lucky? "Yes," she said, "but maybe it'd be better if I go first and then you follow."

He sighed. "Okay, if it makes you more comfortable."

A few minutes later, Grace was making the final touches to the tables for the dinner when there was a shriek behind her.

"Darling!" Pia Katsalos, like a pink-and-blue whirlwind, came sailing across the room and wrapped Grace in an enormous hug. Pia always smelled of cinnamon and spun sugar, and Grace hugged her tightly. "I can't thank you enough for all that you've done while I've been away," Pia said. She stood back and, after wiping tears from her cheeks, swept her arms wide. "And these gorgeous tables, and this incredible room! Between Yasmin and Lane, Nick and Erin, and you, you've all done an incredible job of making the Palace look amazing!"

"It's been a fantastic team effort," Grace said, her heart bursting with pride. "I'm so glad you like it."

"Like it? I *love* it! I know that Nicky has spent so much money on this, and Lane's and Yasmin's influence is obvious in so many of the decorations and the menu, but it's *you*, you're the one who's been the constant here. If it weren't for you, *none* of this would've happened."

"Ari's been a great help in the last week or two," Grace said, aware he hadn't come in for any of Pia's praise.

"Oh, really?" she said, raising an eyebrow. "He is certainly loyal, that boy, but his attitude toward weddings is so disappointing."

There was a noise at the door, and they both turned to see Ari. It was clear he'd have heard his mother, but as he came close and kissed her on both cheeks, he didn't show it.

"You look beautiful, Mom. It's great to have you back here."

Heat rushed to her own cheeks, and she quickly moved away so Pia didn't notice. "It's warm in here," she said quickly. "I'll just open a window or two."

"Hasn't Grace done an amazing job with this place?" Ari said, looking over his mother's head and throwing a wink at Grace.

"It's beautiful," Pia said. "If only Mano and I had been able to agree on making these sorts of changes a long, long time ago, things might have ended differently. Who could've imagined that this old place could turn out like this?"

"I could." They all turned to see Mano walking in. He wore a suit, and his normally unruly hair was carefully brushed to one side. "We should be proud of all that we have done here, Pia. Most especially the wonderful children we have created—and the occasion of Nicky's wedding is a good time for us to remember that."

"Of course, it is," Pia said, not looking at her husband.

"When all my children are settled down with families of their own, then I can rest easy. Grace," she said, "I hope you have brought a date."

Her cheeks flamed hotter still. "I…ah…"

Mano spread his arms wide. "You are joining us tonight as a very important part of our family. Someone who has been loyal and helped us through one of our toughest times. Of course, I would prefer to have you stay on forever and ever, but it will bring me great joy to see you successful in a business of your own." He came over and pulled her into a hug, his cheek damp against her forehead. Was he crying?

Grace looked over at Ari, but he was concentrating on his father, his eyebrows drawn together. "You've lost weight, Pop."

"Bah," Mano said, brushing his eyes. "It is because I am missing your mother's food. Nothing tastes the way it should when it is not cooked by your mother."

Pia gave a small smile. "Just as well you have lost weight. You fit into your old suit again."

"And I had to have one made especially for the wedding," Mano said. "Nicky insisted on buying one for me in Rome."

"Are my ears burning?" Nick came in, hand in hand with Erin, each of them beaming.

"Ah, the guests of honor, you're here!" Pia hurried to kiss them, closely followed by Mano. Ari hugged his brother and kissed his sister-in-law-to-be, and only moments later, Yasmin and Lane arrived. Soon the room was buzzing as everyone caught up with each other.

"Come and catch up with Yasmin and Lane," Ari said, guiding her by the shoulder, and before she could make an excuse about needing to check arrangements, she'd been drawn into a circle with Yasmin, Lane, and Ari and Yasmin's cousin Costa. They were all so good-looking with their olive skin and jet-black hair. Not long now, and they wouldn't be part of her workday, or her life, as she moved on to her own business.

"Lovely to see you again, Grace," Costa said as he leaned in and kissed her first on one cheek and then the other. She'd been around the Katsalos family and their friends long enough to get used to the way Greek people addressed each other, but she still hadn't quite gotten used to the intimacy. Yasmin and Lane leaned in to do the same, and she marveled at how Lane was so much a part of this family already.

"Have you lived in the States?" Grace asked Costa. "Your English is amazing."

"Costa's our most international cousin," Yasmin said as she patted Costa's arm. "Living in Switzerland and jetting back to Lesvos for the summer, then over here to do business, it's hard to keep track of him. We like to call Costa, Markus and Christo the Billionaires of Brentwood Bay, and we feel super privileged when they grace us with their presence."

Costa arched an eyebrow. "Yasmin is too kind and forgets that I was a village boy until I left school. There were plenty of rough edges still until I came and worked at the Palace to improve my English when I was seventeen. Uncle Mano taught me more about business than I ever learned later at university." His charcoal eyes sparkled.

"I know what you mean," Grace said as she looked at first Yasmin, then Ari. "Pia and Mano taught me so much about how to treat clients and how to stay true to your vision. And they always seem to have lots of family working for them, which is lovely. I remember Christo from your grandmother's funeral, and he was here for the relaunch of the Palace when you and Lane were working here. Right, Yasmin?"

"That's right," Yasmin said. "He grew up here, as Markus did. You might not have met him. He's Leo's son and owns a big Turkish delight company in Cyprus."

"Oh, no, I haven't, but I've met his brother Alex a few times. We're looking after his girlfriend's cat at the moment," she said as she looked around for Boris and spied him curled up on a window seat. "Pia said Alex and Mara will be at the wedding, so I guess Boris will be leaving soon. I'm going to miss this whole family when I make the final leap to my own business."

Yasmin reached out and touched her arm, warmth and kindness shining in her eyes. "You deserve every success, Grace. You've done so much for my parents and this place and we're so grateful to you."

Nick joined the group then, and the cousins started talking about being back together and Nick and Erin's wedding.

"Having fun?" Grace said as she picked up a glass of champagne from a passing waiter and handed it to Ari. She turned away from the others so they wouldn't hear her conversation.

Ari leaned in, close to her ear. "I'd be having a whole lot more fun if it was just you and me sharing a glass of wine in my apartment," he whispered.

"How long since you were all together in the one place?" she asked as she drew back and looked into his dark eyes.

He shrugged. "You know, I can't even remember. It would have been an Easter, or Christmas. Probably when my yiayia was still alive. We're a tight family, but we've seen less and less of each other as the years have rolled by."

"You see," she teased. "That's why weddings are so *important*. They give families an excuse to come together unlike any other time."

"And spend all the inheritance on dresses you'll never wear again, and mix with people you'll never talk to."

She leaned a little closer. "If I really believed that, I wouldn't be so good at my job." She breathed deep and waited until he looked back at her. "You know, I truly believe that weddings are an incredibly powerful time in human relationships."

He nodded. "I know that's true for that point in people's lives. It's what happens after the wedding that I don't believe in."

She was quiet for a moment and internally kicked herself for bringing this up. They were never going to agree, and there was no point in her thinking she could convince him.

He was looking around the room and over her head at the groups of people. "What are you thinking about?" she asked.

He dropped his voice and looked her directly in the eye. "That there must be a way I can grab you by the hand and take you away somewhere. Anywhere. So we could be alone and shut out the world and pretend that we could live that way forever. How about you?"

She looked over to where his family were talking and laughing in small groups. Should she tell him the truth? That more and more she was wondering if she was wasting her time. Their time? That she couldn't be with a guy who didn't believe in marriage—it was, quite simply, a deal breaker.

If they had such a fundamental disagreement about commitment, then was there any real point in carrying on? But his touch, and his sweet kisses? She wasn't ready to walk away from those—at least, not yet.

Ari gazed around the table at his family. His mom and Erin were chatting on one side, while his dad and Nick were laughing at a joke in the other. A number of aunts, uncles, and cousins were there, including Leo and his family, along with Erin's parents and her sisters. Grace had asked Lane about his plans for a new restaurant in town, and they were deep in discussion. Yasmin had turned her chair deliberately and was now facing Ari.

"So, we have a plan to finally get Mom and Dad talking," she said in a low voice. "Want to hear it?"

He shrugged and pulled his gaze from Grace. "I dunno. Is it wise to try to intervene again? You guys and Nick and Erin have obviously spent some time with them in Greece, and that hasn't changed anything, and now that the focus is on the wedding, they'll probably be too distracted."

Yasmin leaned back a little in her chair and sighed. "I knew you'd think they were better off apart. Someone as unromantic as you wouldn't see the depth of love they have for each other."

"Don't be ridiculous," he said. "Of course, I want them to both be happy, but check out Mom. She looks ten years younger since she's been in Greece. I don't want to be responsible for making her think she has to come back here just because it makes us happy."

"You're right. She does seem happier, but I'd bet it's because she hasn't had to deal with this place—not because she necessarily wants to be away from Dad."

Ari leaned his elbow on the table. "Okay, what's the great plan to get them back together?"

"Talking Dad into selling the Palace. When he finally agrees to that, then maybe Mom will be able to see a future for them."

"But why should Dad have to do that? This place is part of him. He and Mom have worked at it together. Built it from nothing. Why should she be the one to decide their future?"

"Because compromise is what you do in a relationship," Yasmin said.

"Change each other, you mean." He regretted the words as soon as they were out of his mouth. Tonight was about Erin and Nick, and he didn't need to share his beliefs on the drawbacks of marriage.

"You think that's what Lane and I are doing? Changing each other?"

He should've stayed quiet. This was not the place to argue the negative side of marriage, but he had to make Yasmin see that maybe getting back together wasn't the best thing for their parents.

"You're not married, so it doesn't count. But when you are, I guarantee it'll change you both, and not for the better," he said.

Yasmin sighed, and her tone became sharper. "That job has poisoned you."

He shrugged. "If that's the same as showing me the reality of marriage and confirming that it'll never be something I do in my life, then I'll take being poisoned over being disillusioned any day."

There was a tinkling sound, and they turned their gaze toward Mano, who was standing at the head of the table and tapping a glass with his knife.

"I would like to make some toast," Ari's father said, and Ari's gaze slid to his brother and sister, who each had a quiet smile on their face. Mano's English was usually pretty good, but he occasionally dropped a doozy.

"Firstly, I would like to thank my ancestors who made us Greek, a culture of which we are all so very proud."

Everyone chuckled, and Ari leaned in and whispered into Grace's ear. "You think that's bad? He'll thank Monty for being the best wedding-hall bird ever before this speech is over. Buckle up." She secretly dug him in the ribs with an elbow, but she was trying not to smile.

"Love is not always an easy thing," Mano was saying. "Sometimes it takes all your effort and energy to love someone, but that in itself is an act of love."

Ari reached for Grace's hand under the table cloth and squeezed.

"But the thing that makes all the difference is marriage." Mano took a breath and looked around the table. "When you make the vows on your wedding day, what you are really doing is making a promise that you will choose to love that person every day, no matter what."

Ari groaned inwardly. This was not the time for his father to be talking about his own marriage. Mano should be speaking about Nick and Erin. He turned to where his mother was sitting, but she had a look of calm serenity on her face.

"The real fact is that when you wake up each morning next to your wife or your husband, you must *choose* love. You must always make the conscious decision to love her, and eventually she will see that and realize she can choose to love you too."

There was silence in the room, and then Nick stood, moved toward his father, and embraced him. "Pop, you and Mom have made it so easy for us to learn how to love, and for that I am so very grateful."

Mano brushed the back of his hands across his eyes and then said in a booming voice, "Then we must make some toast!"

Everyone around the table stood and lifted their glasses. "To love," said Mano, and everyone responded, "To love. To toast!"

When everyone was seated again, the noise level rose, and Ari took the opportunity to lean close to Grace, but he spoke in a voice loud enough for those around him to hear. "We need to check the lighting behind the outdoor bar. Now's as good a time as any."

Her eyes rounded, but she put her napkin on the table. "Yes, I guess this is a good opportunity. We won't have time in the next day or two." She turned to Lane on her left and said, "I'll be back in a moment. I just need to check some of the outdoor lighting."

Ari held the door to the courtyard open and stepped outside after her. As soon as he was beside her, he reached for her hand.

"What are you doing?" she said with a laugh in her voice. "Anyone could see us out here. Come away from the light."

She pulled him into the shadows, and he drew her close. "I don't care who knows that we're together," he said. Her warm breath fanned across his face, and even in the half-light, he could see the shine in her eyes. "I want them to see how you make me feel."

She put her hands against his chest and tilted her chin. "But I don't want to tell everyone. While this is still a bit of fun between the two of us, I don't want other people knowing about it."

"Who's a pretty boy? Who's a pretty boy?" Monty's guttural voice only a few yards away made them both start to laugh.

"I keep forgetting how hard it is to get any privacy around this place," Ari said. "I'd put money on Monty giving away our secret before anyone else finds out." He pulled her close and pressed his lips against her mouth. "Have I told you how incredible you look tonight?"

"I think you mentioned it once in my apartment and then once when I passed you a tray of drinks." She laughed. "And maybe I heard you mention it when you bent down to pick up a dropped serviette." He laughed, then kissed a line from her mouth to her ear. She smelled of shampoo and sunshine, and he wanted to bury himself in her. He couldn't remember the last time someone had gotten under his skin like this. In fact, no one had ever filled his mind like she did. He felt wanted, he felt alive, and he wanted it to go on forever.

7

$\mathcal{A}$ few hours later, Ari lay in Grace's bed with her snuggled close against him, her arm around his waist. The full moon through the window caused everything in her room to glow silver—a reflection of the light pulsing inside him right now at being here with her.

"Thanks for tonight," he said in a quiet voice, unsure if she'd already fallen asleep.

"It was beautiful, wasn't it?" she said sleepily, her face illuminated by the moonlight. "Everyone got on so well, and I even saw your mom and dad talking to each other at the end of the night."

She twisted around and rested her head on the pillow so she was now looking directly at him. "How did you feel with everyone back together again?" She stroked his chest. "Was it weird or good?"

"Surprisingly good." He tried to keep his voice steady as the pads of her fingers trailed featherlight across his skin. "I can't believe how much has changed in less than a year—it's like we've all finally grown up. "

"In what sort of way?"

"I guess compared to some families we've always been reasonably close—always trying to be together for Thanksgiving, Christmas, and Easter, which is a huge deal for Greeks. But there was always this distance between my parents and us kids, you know? Not a cold distance, a kind of barrier where they'd always put a great spin on things, never let us see when things were tough, or share the bad times. Was your family like that?"

She was quiet for a second and her hand stilled on his chest. "Not really, no. My parents have always been pretty straight up with us, and I think it meant my brother and I were straight up with them most of the time. In fact, my mom was asking for the truth about how things were between Mark and me way before I was ready to admit it to myself, or her. But that's great that you feel like your parents are being more honest."

"I don't think Dad had much choice when Mom left to go back to Greece; it was all laid bare for everyone to see. I just hope it stays that way."

"I've been wondering something," Grace said as she resumed gently stroking his arm. "Why do you have those words pinned to your walls?"

"Promise you won't laugh?"

Her mouth turned down. "When have I ever laughed at you?"

"Never," he conceded, "but it sounds kinda crazy when I say it out loud."

She gave him one of her sparkling smiles. "Try me."

"I never used to buy people birthday cards because I'd get the words wrong, but then when my sister got sick in Borneo, she didn't tell my parents how sick she was— another example of my family not being straight with each other. Anyway, I wanted to send her something special, more than a typed email, a proper card, saying how much I was rooting for her, so I needed a way to teach myself to write it."

"Oh, that's beautiful," Grace said. "But how did you do it?"

"I listened to a bunch of songs and picked out the words I liked, then I found the lyrics online and copied the words. Ed Sheeran's got some pretty cool lyrics and someone had hand-written them online so I copied them. Crazy, right?"

Grace looked down for a moment, then back at him, her eyes glossy. "It sounds exactly like the sort of thing you'd do."

"Yasmin likes that sort of thing," he said, embarrassed. "Much easier to just phone."

She must've sensed the way he felt because she changed the subject. "Have I told you how much I love these tattoos?" she said, before planting a gentle kiss on his shoulder. "Tell me the story behind them. They're Greek gods, right?"

"Yeah," he said. "I got my first one, Zeus, the big guy in the middle, when I first left home. He's the father of the gods, so I guess it was kind of me carrying a father figure with me when I struck out on my own."

"That's so cool," Grace breathed. "And who are these men and women around him? I don't know much about mytholo-gy." She marked a circle around his heart, and his chest expanded. "His children?"

He held her hand and traced around each of the figures, etched deep into his skin. "On his right, there's Herakles, for his strength, and on his left, Athena and her owl representing wisdom."

"I'm glad you included a woman," she said in a teasing voice.

"She's also a warrior, and I liked the idea of coming from warrior stock."

"And below them?" Her voice was lower, sexier.

"That's Atlas." The warmth of her honey-breath against his skin was almost too much to bear.

"Just like you."

He chuckled. "You think I have some things in common with Atlas? My godlike looks perhaps?"

She laughed then spoke more quietly. "Carrying the world on your shoulders, maybe."

He hugged her closer.

"I can see your strength in them. How you carry loyalty and duty around with you," she said.

He nodded. "Yeah, but they didn't stumble through life like I've done. They were worthy and strong."

"You're more than worthy," she said as she moved her hand lower.

"Hearing you say it makes me wish it were true." He didn't mean it to sound the way it did, but he wasn't hiding anything from Grace anymore.

She propped up on her elbow, resting her head on her hand. "You know what I just realized?" she said, moonlight splashing across her face.

"What's that?"

"Your gods are kind of like my star signs."

"How do you mean?" he asked, linking his fingers through her free hand.

"Maybe we're both looking for some guidance on how we should navigate our way in the world."

He kissed her forehead. "You know, when I first heard you talking about star signs and character traits, I thought you liked to put people in boxes. But maybe you're right. Maybe we've both been trying to find out more about ourselves."

"Funny," she said, as he kissed her ear. "That's exactly what I thought about you when we first met. That you put people in boxes, wanted them all to be the same. But now that I know the real you, I can see that's not true at all." She moved closer and soon their bodies were intertwined again.

"Who'd have thought," she whispered in his ear, "that a guy who I imagined was my complete opposite would help me know myself better than I ever had before."

*Saturday August 19th*

Grace looked at the clock on her office wall and breathed a sigh of relief. Thirty minutes until the Williams wedding began. This was the point of no return. As it was in all the weddings she'd ever planned, there was a point in the day when the clock would race, a time when there was nothing more she could do. The day would go ahead now, and she had to trust that everything would be perfect. She'd coached Polly to take things from here while she rushed over to Patterson's, but she could get back to the Palace if anything went wrong.

What would be going on there right now? Erin and Nick's wedding wasn't for another three hours, but everything would be frantic. Would Erin be having her hair and makeup done? Would Nick be doing some final practice for his speech?

Ari would be working in his office, not really interested in his brother's wedding, but ready to show up for the sake of his family. They'd spent a wonderful week together, catching intimate moments during their busy days and spending secret hours together at night. Whenever they were apart, her head was filled with him, and she couldn't wait until this day was over so they could really spend time together.

She'd popped her head around the kitchen door to check with Pavlo that everything was okay, when there was a commotion behind her.

*"Koukla-mou!"* Pia came rushing toward her with curlers in her hair, a phone clutched in her hand. She wore a brightly

colored, oversize kaftan and bare feet. Her face was white and her voice shaky.

"Grace, I know you are so busy today, but I really need your help."

"What is it?" she asked, pulling over a chair and guiding Pia into it. "Are you ill? Here, take my hand." She reached for Pia's hand, and the older woman squeezed hard.

"Nicky just called me," she said as she struggled for breath. "Ari has had an accident on his motorcycle on the way from his office—"

Grace's heart seized in her chest. "Oh my God, is he okay?"

"That is the thing, I don't know. It was a passerby who called Nicky. At least, I'm hoping that Ari was conscious enough to give him a number to call. But maybe he just rang the first number he could find in Ari's phone. I don't know!" she wailed. "I made Nicky promise he wouldn't go to Ari. That he would let me find out what was going on so the wedding doesn't need to be interrupted."

Cold sweat crawled down Grace's neck. "Do you know where the accident was?"

"By the Episcopalian church. The man told Nicky that a car ran a red light. Leo has been using my car while I've been in Greece, so there's no way for me to get there. Do you think I could borrow yours?"

"Oh, Pia, I don't have a car, remember?" As the words came out her mouth, she was riddled with shame and anger that she couldn't help Ari or Pia at such a critical moment. Why had she believed Mark when he'd said she shouldn't be let loose on the roads? "Does Mano know about the accident?"

"I don't know," Pia said. "I came straight down here."

"If an ambulance has been called, he might already have been taken to hospital, so why don't we let Mano know and then call the hospital." As she was saying the words, she cursed herself for not having the courage to own a car and Ari for riding that death machine. She ached to be with him, to hold him and tell him that he made her feel strong and capable and she didn't know what she would do if she lost him.

The phone in Pia's hand rang, and she quickly swiped the accept button and put the phone to her ear.

Grace's mind raced as she tried to work out how she could get to Ari. She'd promised she'd be back at Patterson's by three, but maybe Nick and Erin's wedding would need to be postponed anyway. Her mind was spinning.

"Yes," Pia was saying on the phone. "Yes, of course. I'll wait outside." She put the phone down. "It was Mano. He's coming straight here to get me. He says the ambulance is with Ari, so we will go straight there."

"Did he say anything about how Ari is?" Grace said, trying not to show her desperation for some positive news.

"No, he had only spoken to the man who called Nicky." She patted Grace's arm. "You have so much to do here. Don't worry."

Not worry? Bile rose in the back of her throat, and she steadied herself against the wall.

"You've done more than enough for my family," Pia said. "I'm sure everything will be fine. As soon as I have some news, I'll let you know."

She hurried off, and Grace stood frozen. How could she carry on when all she could think about was being by Ari's side? But she didn't have the right to do that. She'd been the one pushing to keep their relationship secret, and what might it now cost her?

Maybe it was simple. Watching Pia go through the gate, she lifted her chin. She couldn't go on pretending there wasn't anything between them, and why should she, anyway?

Ari made her feel strong and capable. He'd understood why she didn't want to reveal their relationship to his family, and he hadn't pushed her on it.

Yes, her business was important to her, but none of that mattered if she didn't have him in her life. And what if he was lying unconscious in a hospital bed, unaware of what he really meant to her? She *had* to be with him. She reached into her pocket and pulled out her phone. There was nowhere she wanted to be more than by Ari's side at the hospital. For the hundredth time, she cursed herself for not having a car and clicked on the Uber app.

The screen flashed to show a call was coming in. It could be Nick with more news. She slid the button to accept.

"Hey." The second her brain registered Ari's voice, her body was awash with adrenaline.

"Oh my God," she said as her free hand flew to her mouth. Her legs were jelly, her heart tripping. "Are you okay? Are you hurt? Do they need to take you to the hospital?"

"You heard I had a little disagreement with a blue Chevy?" He chuckled. "I'm fine. Just a few scrapes. My bike's a lot worse off than I am, though. I'm getting the paramedic to clean me up, and then I'll head over to Patterson's."

The whole of her body shook, and she sank into the nearest chair.

"Grace, are you there?"

"Yes…I…" The words wobbled in her mouth, and she bit her lip.

"I'm sorry. I know you're busy. I should've sent a text instead. What I really wanted to say was good luck for the weddings today. I know you've been working so hard to get everything right, and it's going to be incredible."

She dragged breath into her lungs. "Of course, you should've called me," she said. "I was just about to get an

Uber to come over there. I can still do it if you need me. Polly can take care of things here."

"You were?" he said.

"Of course! Oh, Ari I had visions of you unconscious, never being able to walk again—or worse."

"They couldn't get my helmet off so I couldn't call anyone," he said. "I thought about texting, but knew that would probably bring the whole family running. I asked a guy who stopped to help if he could call Nick for me and let him know I'd be late."

"Stay there, and I'll call a cab and come get you," she said, trying to keep desperation out of her voice.

"I'm fine, honestly," he said. "I'll need to get to Patterson's before they postpone the wedding. Mom and Dad are on their way here, so I'll have a ride."

"Okay," she said. "But I'm going to meet you there. I want to see for myself that you're okay." Her voice cracked then. She could've blamed the pressure of running two weddings in one day, or the frustration that she'd lost confidence and couldn't drive anywhere, but deep down she knew the real reason was she couldn't stand it if Ari was hurt.

"Sweetheart, it's going to be fine," he said in a soft voice. There was silence for a moment. "Trust me to screw up the most important day for my family and for you."

"You haven't screwed anything up," she said fiercely as she brushed her hand across her cheek. "You always put everyone else's needs before your own." She drew in a breath, and for the shortest moment wondered if she should say what was really in her heart. The words came out before she could make a decision. "Your family loves you, and none of our lives would be the same if anything happened to you."

There was silence for a beat, and then two. She'd said too much, gotten carried away in the emotion of the moment.

"I have to go. Mom and Dad are here. I'll see you soon."

When he'd hung up, Grace stared at her phone. She was glad she'd said what she had. Ari was important to everyone in his family, and in the last few weeks, he'd become the most important person in her life. When she did see him next, she'd lay her heart on the line, tell him what he meant to her, too, and maybe then he could see that they could have a real future together.

~

Ari sat in a room at Patterson's Weddings with both his mother and sister fussing around him, his left leg sticking straight out in front of him in a moon boot. The paramedics had said he should have an X-ray, but there would be time enough for that tomorrow. His father sat in a corner reading through his speech. The wedding had been postponed for half an hour so his parents could get ready after their unexpected detour, and all he wanted to do was go and find Grace.

"I'm okay, Mom," he said as his mother dabbed at a cut under his eye where the helmet had been crushed. "Yas, will you take her out into the garden or something?"

"I'm not going anywhere," his mother said as she patted his arm. "I always knew something would happen to you on that bike. If only I had come in a car to get you, you wouldn't have had to ride that wretched thing. I blame myself for all this," she continued. "If I hadn't left—"

"Pia, come with me," Mano said as he stood. "You need to be calm for the wedding. Seeing your eldest son get married? This is one of the greatest days of your life, and you deserve to worry about nothing else. Yasmin will make sure Ari is fine."

His mother stopped dabbing Ari's cheek and handed the Kleenex to her daughter. "Just make sure it's covered," she said as she patted her son's arm again. "We don't want anyone thinking you've been in another one of your fights. And how are you going to walk on that leg? Will we need to have a wheelchair in the front row?"

"I'm okay, Mom. Just go and enjoy the wedding. I'll be fine."

His father held the door open for his mother, and Ari smiled at his sister. He'd noticed a closeness between his parents when they'd both come to see him at the accident site. His mom liked to make out that he exasperated her, but when she first got there she'd kissed him and told him she wouldn't know what to do if anything happened to him. When she'd stepped away, Mano had held her hand, and they were still like that when the paramedics had helped Ari into their car.

"You saw that too?" Yasmin asked as she lifted her hand to dab something on Ari's cheek.

He gently pushed her hand away and rearranged his jacket. "Mom smiling at Pop when he opened the door for her? I swear they were laughing when they first arrived here. Pop drove Mom back to the Palace so she could finish getting ready. Maybe they had time to do some talking?"

There was a light tap at the door. When it opened, Grace put her head around. "Okay if I come in?"

Every one of Ari's muscles strained to be near her, but she wouldn't want that in front of his sister.

"Ari's fine," Yasmin said to her. "You must be so busy right now. Don't worry, I'll take care of him."

"Lane's looking for you," Grace said. "I think it was something about a corsage for your mom...?"

Yasmin looked first at Ari and then at Grace. "Oh, okay," she said, smiling slowly. "I'd better make sure that gets sorted out. Will you be okay to get Ari to the ceremony, Grace?"

"I think I'll manage," she said with a grin.

When Yasmin had gone, Grace drew near but didn't get close enough. She had an earpiece in and was dressed in a formal blue suit.

"Are you okay?" he asked, worried that he'd made her day all the more stressful. "You shouldn't be in here worrying about me when you've got so much to do here and back at the Palace."

She stepped closer, and he could see there were tears in her eyes. "Don't do that to me again," she whispered, her lip trembling. "You probably think I'm just emotional and stressed because I had so much riding on today, but you know what?" She drew in a deep breath. He tried to stand up, but she was beside him in an instant. "No, don't. Please."

"Hey, what is it? What's wrong?" he asked as he stroked her arm.

"I just don't know what I'd do—" She gulped. "I don't think I can handle the thought of you riding that bike any longer."

Ari opened his mouth and then closed it. Had she really said that? He sat straighter in the chair. "Honey, it wasn't the bike that was the problem, it was the driver of the car."

"*Promise* me," she said as she threw her arms around his neck. "Promise me you'll put the bike away."

Ari stilled. "I'm fine," he said. "Honestly, it wasn't my fault, and nobody was really hurt." This wasn't the Grace he knew talking.

She leaned in and kissed him on the lips, and he could hear her intake of breath as their skin touched.

"Hey, Grace," he said as he pulled her away. "What is it?"

Her eyes were glossy and her face pale. "Hearing that you'd had an accident made me realize what you mean to me."

It was the stress of the weddings talking. Later on, she

would be back to the confident, in control Grace he had fallen for.

"I'm glad the thought of me being laid up didn't give you an easy out," he said, trying to make a joke.

Her face was still serious, so he held her chilled hands. "I'm not going anywhere, Grace. Whether you like it or not, I'm going to be around for a while yet." Her dusky pink lips tilted in a watery smile, but the look on her face still unsettled him.

"I should go," she said. "And so should you. The ceremony will begin in half an hour."

"All the best," he said. "I know you'll make Nick and Erin's day perfect." She leaned down and kissed him firmly, and he cupped her face as he kissed her back.

"When can I see you again?" she whispered. "Tonight?"

"You'll be too busy, won't you? And I guess I should really get some rest. Why don't you come by tomorrow night?"

"It'll be late tonight," she conceded. "And I guess you'll want to go to the barbecue Erin's parents are putting on here tomorrow."

"You know I'd come and get you tomorrow if my leg wasn't banged up," he said.

"I know." She smiled, a real Grace smile this time. "You don't have a spare key, do you? So I don't have to wake you up?"

First, she was telling him she didn't want him riding his motorcycle, and now she wanted a key to his apartment? When had she started to care about him so much?

"Sure," he said, reaching into his jacket pocket. He removed his key from the keyring and handed it to her. "I'll call the janitor and tell him I've lost my keys. He'll let me in."

"Thanks," she said. "I'll see you tomorrow night." She waggled her fingers at him before she turned the door handle. "I'll send Yasmin in to collect you. Have a wonderful time at the wedding."

"Oh, I'm sure I will," he said with a grin.

"Just don't spend too much time dancing with those bridesmaids." She gave him a cheeky grin. "Maybe I am glad you can't walk." That was the Grace he knew.

"I'll spend all my time thinking of you coming to my bed tomorrow night," he said.

She blew him a kiss and was gone.

Ari stared at the closed door and tried to ignore the icy sense of dread beginning to run through his veins. Something had shifted between him and Grace just now. For a few moments, the fun and the laughter and the sheer thrill of being together had been replaced with expectation and assumption, and it didn't sit right. Not right at all. He wanted the confident Grace back, the one who liked him to be daring and carefree, the one who was independent and strong and lived for the here and now.

She cared about him, that was clear—more than he imagined possible—but how he felt about that, he wasn't so sure.

8

The next evening, Ari sat on a chair in his apartment with his leg balanced on a couple of cushions on the coffee table. It hurt like hell, but he wouldn't be taking any pain meds. He'd had a lead on Tony Partella for weeks, and now that the cheating businessman was back in Brentwood Bay, Ari wanted to stay clearheaded in case he had the chance to follow him. Of course, not being able to ride his bike was a problem, but he'd work something out. It was nine thirty, and he was just contemplating calling it a night, when a key turned in his lock.

A second later, the door swung open, and there was Grace. In an instant, his pain was forgotten as he drowned in her gorgeous smile and sparkling face. She carried a large brown supermarket sack and a carry bag, and he cursed the fact he couldn't race over and scoop her into his arms.

"Hey!" She beamed.

"Well, you're a sight for sore legs," he said as she made her way over to him. He struggled to sit up taller.

"You just stay right there, mister," she said, then leaned down and pressed her lips against his. He pulled her close, and for a moment he couldn't care whether he lived or died, as long as he stayed right here, with her.

"Oi!" she said, struggling free and pulling the paper bag from between them like a rabbit out of a hat. "There's some very expensive fillet steak in there!"

He grabbed the bag, put it on the floor, and pulled her to him again. "Who cares about steak," he said. "God, I've missed you."

She peppered his face with tiny kisses, then tucked her hands inside his shirt and slid her palms across his skin. "Not as much as I've missed you. And now the weddings are over, we can spend every single minute together. In fact," she said with a cheeky smile, "I quite like the fact you can only hobble around. It means I can stay here and nurse you, and you can't get away."

"Hmmm," he said, trying to keep his voice steady as she dragged her fingertips lightly across his shoulders. He faked a serious tone. "I'm pretty sure the doctors would prefer it if I stayed in bed all day."

"Then we certainly agree on that." She kissed him long and deep. "And if you're trapped on the couch," she said, gazing around the room, "maybe I can have a go at tidying up around here. I don't know how you find anything."

"You won't need to find anything but me," he said as he squeezed her hands. "Come and tell me how the wedding went for the congressman's daughter."

She laughed. "I can't quite believe we pulled it off. I probably overdid the organization and hired too many extra people, but it meant we didn't have one single issue, and everyone seemed to be really happy."

"I know Erin and Nick said their day was great thanks to everything you did."

"Are you hungry?" she said as she laid another kiss at the corner of his mouth.

"Starving. I would say only for you, but you're probably being deafened by my growling stomach right now." He winced at the open jar of peanut butter sat on the coffee table with a spoon sticking out of it.

"Peanut butter? Straight out of the jar. Really?"

"It hurt to stand at the cook top," he said with puppy-dog eyes.

She patted his cheek. "I'm going to teach you how to cook, remember? Seems we can't get this leg better quick enough." She picked up the paper sack and moved toward the kitchen. "Did Nick and Erin get away on their honeymoon okay?" she asked over her shoulder, picking up a few coffee cups along her way.

He twisted on the chair, trying to ignore her second dig about his lack of order. "I guess so. I only stayed for a couple of hours yesterday. My leg was hurting pretty bad. Mom and Dad dropped me home early."

"I've just seen your mom and dad back at the Palace," Grace said as she got things out of the bag and laid them on the counter. "They were sitting out in the garden, talking over a cup of coffee. They seemed pretty deep in conversation."

He raised his eyebrows. "They seemed to be talking lot at Erin and Nick's wedding as well."

She smiled. "How do you think things are going between them?" She pulled things out of the cupboards.

"I really don't know. I guess they could either be deciding the Palace's fate, or be thinking about coming back here to work on their marriage."

The front door buzzer sounded.

"Are you expecting anyone?" Grace asked, her voice wary.

"Don't think so. I'm waiting on some information about a guy I've been following, but I haven't told anyone to come here with it. Can you answer on the intercom for me?"

She turned and her eyes widened. "What if it's one of your family?"

"It won't be. As you said, Nick and Erin will have gone, and Mom and Dad were at the Palace. Yasmin said she had some friends to catch up with today. Don't be so worried. Even if it is, it wouldn't be the end of the world if one of them found you here."

Grace hesitated, but finally walked over to the intercom and pushed the button. "Hello."

There was silence for a moment before a female voice said, "Oh, I'm sorry. I must have the wrong apartment. I'm looking for Ari Katsalos."

"Yasmin, it's Grace." She turned to him, her face pale. "You do have the right apartment. I just came to check on how Ari was after his accident."

"Can I come in?" There was a smile in his sister's voice, and it was obvious she knew. But what did it matter anyway? Grace would soon be leaving the Palace. It shouldn't matter if his family knew they were dating.

"Of course." Grace pushed the buzzer and hung up the handset.

"Do you think she's figured it out?" she asked, her face stony.

"Yes, but it's fine. The weddings are over, and you're not an employee. It shouldn't matter who knows that we're together." She was silent but moved to the door and opened it to Yasmin. They greeted each other with a hug.

"Hey big bro, how's it going?" Yasmin asked as she came through the door carrying a very large box. "And how lucky are you to have Grace around to nurse you?"

"I'm extremely lucky," he said with a smile. "And it's nice not to have to hide the fact that Grace and I are seeing each other."

Grace was standing, stunned. She'd probably have

preferred to wait until things were more serious between them, but as far as he was concerned, they already were.

"Well, as it was one of the most popular topics of conversation yesterday at the wedding, I'm glad we were all right," Yasmin said cheerily. She moved into the kitchen, put the box on the counter, and gave Grace another hug. "I personally think it's fantastic news."

"How long have you known?" Grace asked, throwing Ari a glare from over his sister's shoulder.

"It was pretty obvious when we had the family dinner, but your visit to him at Patterson's on the day of the wedding confirmed it for me. I'm really happy for you both."

"Do your parents know?" Grace asked hesitantly.

"It was Pop who first mentioned it when you and Ari went outside at the Palace dinner. It was also Pop who insisted I bring over a box of leftover food for you, Ari. But I can see that you're being very well looked after."

"Will you stay and eat with us?" Grace asked.

Yasmin brushed her hands down her jeans. "No, I can't stay, sorry. Lane is in the car out front. We're going into the city for dinner, and I can't be late."

"I'll be in touch," Ari said. "I've got a bit of work on again, but I guess Mom and Dad will want a family dinner before everyone goes their separate ways again."

"Yes, well, I don't think you should be moving around much on that leg," his sister said. "Take a load off for a while. The philanderers will still be philandering when you can walk again." She moved to the door and held up her hand in a wave. "Be good, you two. And maybe I'll see you tomorrow."

After she was gone, there was a moment's silence before Grace spoke. "How do you think they'll really feel about us being together?"

The kitchen counter was a barrier between them, and she stayed fixed behind it.

"I don't really care. I'm proud to be with you, and that's all that matters," he said quietly.

She brushed a piece of hair off her face but said nothing.

"Will you come here?" he asked, holding out an arm to her. Damn this leg. He hated being restricted. He swung it over the side of the coffee table, wincing with the pain.

Immediately, she was by his side. "Don't do that," she scolded. "You'll do yourself more damage."

He snagged her hand and tugged her gently toward the couch. "Sit with me?"

She sat, still with her hand in his.

When she turned to him, he took her other hand. "Grace, I think you know me well enough by now to understand I don't like sneaking around, and not telling my family about us felt like I was lying to them." She dropped her chin.

He squeezed her fingers, and she looked up into his eyes.

"What I don't understand is why you're so against it? Why do you care so much about what people think?"

She squeezed his hands back. "Because I don't want to waste anyone's time."

He let out a chuckle, but she wasn't laughing. "What do you mean?"

She squared her shoulders a little. "I know we said this would just be a bit of fun, but things have changed. I've realized I want more than that."

Ari twined his fingers through hers and smiled the smile that was always the undoing of her. It was a reflection of his strength and his sexiness, his sense of humor and his certainty about his place in the world.

"And why does my family knowing about us change that?"

She swallowed as she tried to get her thoughts straight.

And that was the problem. She didn't think straight around Ari. He made her lose her senses, lose focus on everything else that was important to her, and she didn't like it.

Yes, they'd agreed on this being a casual thing, but now she wanted more. Every moment she was away from him she imagined his touch, remembered the way her head tucked so neatly under his chin when they snuggled. What had been so important to her when she'd left Mark—to re-establish her identity, to make a secure and long-lasting relationship a priority—all seemed to go out the window when Ari was around.

"I guess," she said, searching desperately for the words, "your family knowing about us makes it real, puts us under a pressure we haven't had before."

His hands were warm wrapped around hers. "Are you sure it's not a pressure you've put on yourself?"

"What do you mean?"

"Grace, I know you were deeply hurt by Mark." His voice was a soft caress against the inner pain.

She stilled. "I thought I hid it well."

"I see the pain in your eyes when you mention your marriage. The lack of confidence you have around certain things. And I know you want the next relation-ship you're in to be completely different. And it is. It will be."

She pulled a long breath into her lungs and let it out slowly. "I frighten myself when I'm with you."

He sat rigid. "You're scared of me?"

"No, it's not you. I'm frightened by the way I lose myself when I'm around you. I find myself wanting to be with you all the time. I think about a future with you...all the time."

His lips tilted in a soft smile. "And that's so terrible because...?"

"Because I know you don't believe in marriage." There,

she'd said it. It was out in the open and pulsing like the terrible truth it was.

"That doesn't mean I can't see myself being with you long term." His face was so open and caring, and she wanted to believe everything he said. "Grace, I love the way you make me feel, the way you give me a strength I never knew I needed." He squeezed her hands. "You've made me face some of my worst fears and given me the strength to deal with them. Why wouldn't I want a long-term relationship with you? Marriage is nothing more than a piece of paper. It doesn't define love or commitment."

*Nothing more than a piece of paper?*

A buzzing sound on the table drew Ari's attention away from her, and Grace was grateful for the distraction. She didn't want Ari to see the hollowness in her heart or for him to say something that could make this any more real.

"I'm really sorry. I have to get this," he said.

"Would you like me to leave so you can talk in private?"

"No, no. It won't take a minute."

He let go of one of her hands to reach forward and pick up his phone. "Rick," he answered it and then was silent.

She watched the way his forehead crumpled when he frowned. The way his eyes sparked when the person on the other end obviously said something that excited him. All while he still held her other hand. She was glad their conversation had been interrupted. She needed to stay in the present, enjoy the time she had with Ari, and not think about the future.

"No, it's fine," Ari was saying. "You stay there and keep monitoring, and I'll go to the restaurant. If he's there with her, then we can get some pictures and wrap this up." He was silent for a moment more before he said, "Later," and ended the call.

"Work?" she asked, glad her voice was back to normal.

He shuffled on the chair. "Yeah, and I'm afraid I'm going to have to go out."

"That's okay," she said, relieved to have an excuse to end their talk. "But how will you get there? Will Rick pick you up? You can't ride your bike in this condition."

"That's the tricky bit," he said as he bent to pick up a crutch. "My bike's in the shop anyway. Rick's monitoring the guy's house, in case they decide to go back there early. If I leave now though, I can probably get to the restaurant where they're having dinner before they leave."

"You can't go by taxi, that'd be too obvious," she said. "Why don't we get an Uber? I can come with you and help you get in and out?"

"No, I don't want any possibility of being traced. My neighbor has a car. We could borrow that."

"But you can't drive either," she said.

His mouth slowly tipped up in a grin.

"Oh no, Ari. Not at night." Her chest tightened, and the acid burn of bile stung the back of her throat. "I haven't even tried during the day—"

"You could absolutely do it," he said. "I'll be right there with you."

"And what would we do?" Her mouth dried. "Not some sort of crazy car chase."

"No, nothing like that. We'd just go to the restaurant parking lot, find them, photograph them, and then come back again."

She chewed her thumbnail, trying desperately to think of another way they could do this.

"Please, Grace. I wouldn't ask unless it was really important to me. We can be back here in an hour, sipping on wine and eating fillet steak. You do have a license, right?"

His work was really important to him, and she really did

owe him after everything he'd done to help her in the last few weeks.

"Yes, I have a license… So, we just drive there, get the pictures, drive back, and that's it?" she asked hopefully.

He grinned, and his smile seemed to light the whole of her insides. "Yep, that's all, and we'd better get moving."

~

Grace stood on the pavement and fiddled with the keys in her hand. Ari's neighbor had been more than happy to loan him his car.

"Babe, I don't want to hurry you, but we need to get there before they finish dinner or we could lose him again," Ari said.

Grace pushed down the fear that had flooded her body since she'd agreed to drive. Apparently, it was an automatic, which was some small comfort, but the thought of being behind a steering wheel again made her hands clammy.

"Let me help you in," Ari said as he hobbled toward the driver's door.

"Don't be silly. You're the one who needs a hand," she said as she took his elbow.

She guided him around to the passenger door, held his crutches while he folded himself into the seat, and then tucked the crutches down beside him. "Do we need Google Maps?" she asked as she was ready to close the door.

"No, I know the way."

Moments later, she was sitting in the driver's seat, trying to remember the sequence she needed to follow. "Will you talk to me?" she asked as, hands damp with sweat, she reached for her seat belt and clicked it in. "Sing the alphabet if you need to, just something to calm my brain."

"Of course, I'll talk to you if that's what you want," Ari said. "I just thought you'd prefer to concentrate on the road."

"That was the problem with Mark," she said as she turned the key in the ignition. "He would be silent, watching every move I made, criticizing everything I did. That's what paralyzed me."

He put his hand on hers, and she turned to him. "I'm here for you, Grace. There's no need to be afraid anymore."

She took a lungful of air and smiled at him. "Tell me about this person we're following tonight." She flicked the indicator and looked in the rearview mirror.

"His name's Tony Partella," Ari said. "His wife came to me last year, certain he was having an affair, but it's taken me this long to get the evidence she needed."

"Go on." Ari's voice was soothing her. The fact that he fully trusted her gave her strength, and the thrill of them being a team was empowering.

"My guy Rick's been following him while I've been busy up here, and turns out he has a girlfriend in Brentwood Bay. His wife is in Washington, DC, on business, and Tony's supposed to be tucked up in his own place in the city."

"How did his wife find out?" She stopped the car at a red light, and the adrenaline pump subsided in her body.

"The same way most partners do," Ari said.

The light turned green, and Grace started to move the car forward.

"Watch out for the guy in front. He's about to slow for someone crossing."

Grace's heart leaped into her throat as she slammed her foot on the brake.

"It usually comes from a gut feeling—thinking your partner's cheated."

The pulse in Grace's neck was racing, but Ari was calmly

carrying on with the conversation. She sat higher in her seat and accelerated.

"Lots of people just ignore that intuition, but I'd say it's correct ninety percent of the time."

"The poor wife," Grace said.

"And the girlfriend, or boyfriend. Most of the time they know the cheater is married, but there's always a story about their marriage almost being over, or them having to let their spouse down gently for the sake of the kids."

"Why do you think people do that?" she asked, genuinely wanting to know.

"There's an old song that my dad used to sing years ago— 'The Stranger' by Billy Joel. You know it?" he asked.

She shook her head.

"It's about people never showing their real selves. How we're too scared to show people what we're really like because we're afraid of rejection. And then it all becomes a big web of lies, and one day, when the real person comes out, it's like you have a stranger standing in front of you. You're doing great, by the way."

She smiled. "It's much easier with you in the car."

"Just a left turn here, and then we'll be at the restaurant," Ari said.

"That's a pretty sad view of the world," she said as she pulled into the parking lot, an overwhelming sense of pride washing over her.

Ari shrugged. "It's just reality. We only want people to see our good side. Just pull in here," he said. "I have his license plate details. All we have to do is find a red Audi, and we'll be right."

"There's an Audi over there," Grace said as she switched off the engine.

Ari was flicking through his phone. "Yep, that's the one. All we need to do now is wait."

9

―――――

*S*ilence filled the confines of the car as Ari's words played over in Grace's head. His neighbor must be a smoker, as the air carried the scent of stale smoke, and she rolled down a window to breathe. "Do you think we're like that?" she asked. "Only showing a carefully designed face to each other?" She dragged in a breath of fresh air and held it deep.

"Of course we are," Ari said as he lifted a case from the floor and undid the buckles. "But we're still new, so it doesn't have the power it would if we'd been together longer." He pulled a camera from the case and took off the lens cover.

What did he mean by that? Before she could ask, there was movement at the restaurant door. A young woman in a red coat walked out. Her hair was a wild blonde cloud around her head, and there was something oddly familiar about her.

She walked quickly across the parking lot. Wasn't she the wife of one of Yasmin's friends?

"That's her," Ari said as she moved toward a green

convertible. He lifted the camera to his eye and began click-ing. "Watch the door, he'll come out soon."

"But that's Carmel," Grace said, her fingers over her lips.

"You know her?"

The woman now had her head down, but it was still obvious who she was.

"Indirectly. She married Paul, a friend of Yasmin's. Paul really wanted to get married at the Palace. They came and had a look, but Carmel's mother is friends with Mrs. Patter-son, so they had it there." She turned to Ari, her voice a whisper as she realized what was unfolding in front of her. "They seemed so happy. And their wedding would've been less than a year ago. Yasmin and Lane went and had a great time."

"Here he comes," Ari said. He lifted the camera to his eye again and started clicking very quickly.

The man was dressed in a dark suit. His slightly graying hair was impeccably groomed, and he oozed wealth. He was some distance behind Carmel, but he was watching her, following her. He joined Carmel at the car and touched her on the rear before opening the door for her.

"That is definitely Tony Partella," Ari said, still busy with the camera.

"I just can't believe it." She turned back to Ari. "They seemed so in love, so relaxed and into each other before the wedding. And now…Paul's going to be devastated."

"I've got enough," Ari said.

Grace turned to him. "So, what happens from here?"

He started to put the camera back into its case, seemingly unfazed by Carmel's story. "Now I make up a report for Tony's wife, give her all the evidence, including these photos, and she'll do what she wants with it. As far as cases go, this one's pretty open and shut. By the way Tony's conducting this out in the open, not really going to too much effort to hide his behavior, I'd guess he won't be that upset when his wife finds out."

"And what is his wife likely to do with your photos?" Grace wondered if this was all a mistake. Maybe Carmel was one of the man's work colleagues. The pat on her bottom indicated at least some level of culpability on his part though.

"Well, usually when a partner's prepared to pay for my services, it means they're willing to follow through, but not always."

"What do you mean?" She reeled back as if she were in some alternate universe where what she thought was reality was just smoke and mirrors.

Ari did up the last clip on the camera case and placed it at his feet. He turned to her with the same businesslike look he'd worn since they'd started on this mission. "I've had one guy hire me three times already, and each time, I've found his wife with a different guy. Once I followed her to Florida, another time to Alaska. Unlike Tony here, it seemed like she didn't want to be found out, but she left enough clues along the way that she was pretty easy to bust."

"What sort of clues?" It didn't feel completely right to be asking about the personal lives of these people, but she had to know more, had to hope that somewhere there would be a happy ending. "What happened when you gave her husband the evidence?"

"Happens," Ari corrected her. "It's still going on. Each time I hand him new information, he confronts her, they have an emotional reunion where she promises not to do it again, and then six months later I get another call from him."

"I wonder why he stays," Grace said, as much to herself as to Ari.

He didn't reply, but she could tell he had his own theories.

"What do you think his reasons are?"

Ari shrugged. "He's forgotten how to live his life. He's

become so dependent on her, he's lost belief in himself, or at least in the vision of himself as a happy person."

Carmel pulled out of the restaurant parking lot, and Grace watched while the guy made his way over to his Audi.

"Any kids?" she asked quietly.

"Tony, you mean? Just one. A baby boy. I'm pretty sure his wife will leave him after she sees this, but you never know."

Grace's heart beat low and deep in her chest. No wonder Ari didn't believe in marriage. Day after day, he dealt with lies and deception and the destruction of a happily-ever-after. What chance did she have to convince him there could be an alternative outcome?

"Have there been *any* happy endings?" she asked, not really sure she wanted the answer.

"Happy as in the original couple got back together?" Ari shrugged. "I really don't know. I've heard from a few afterward who say they've never been happier now they're single again."

Grace looked out the window and wished she'd never witnessed Carmel in this situation. Somehow, she almost felt complicit in deceiving Paul, and she didn't want to feel this way ever again.

"We can go now." Ari threw her a smile as he fastened his seat belt. He was so calm and untouched—as if he hadn't just witnessed the dissolution of a marriage—and it bothered her.

She rolled her lips together, still watching the man get into the Audi. "Sure," she said and started the engine.

Before she could put the car in drive, he touched her hand. "Grace, what is it?"

She paused, wondering whether now was the right time to say this. Taking her hands off the wheel, she turned to him. "I *believe* in what I do."

His forehead crumpled, but he gave her a full smile. "Sorry?"

She pulled in a breath then let it all out in a rush. "I wouldn't be in the wedding business if I thought it wasn't important. If I didn't believe that there are thousands of people out there who do take their vows seriously, I wouldn't get up to go to work every day."

He nodded and leaned closer so their mouths were only inches apart. "I get that."

"No, I don't think you do," she said. "I think you imagine I have some fantasy in my head that can never be realized, but it's not like that at all."

Instead of answering her, he leaned in and placed his lips on hers, and for a moment, the drug of his closeness seemed to calm her swirling head. As she kissed him back, she felt herself falling into him, but she stopped and pulled back. "The thing that makes me get up in the morning is thinking —no—*knowing* the lives of these two people are going to be stronger, deeper, and more magnificent because they've made a public declaration to the people who are the most dear to them."

He leaned back against his seat but still held her gaze. "And I would argue that it's precisely the marriage event that causes all the problems. It's like people get into some kind of ownership situation, and they start telling their husband or wife what to do, who to be." He touched her hand and spoke more softly. "I could be wrong, but isn't that exactly what happened in your marriage?"

The air in the car chilled. "That wasn't because we got married. That was a direct result of Mark being a controlling narcissist." She didn't want the failure of her own marriage to be more evidence for Ari's theory. "If I hadn't been blinded by the chemistry that was going on between us, then I might've been able to see him for who he truly was before we got married."

Ari put a hand on hers again and smiled. "We don't have

to agree on this. We can still live our lives, be together even, without agreeing on this."

His deep caramel gaze stayed on her as she swallowed her reply. No, they couldn't go on if this major disagreement lay between them. It was everything she was about, everything she believed in, and if he didn't agree with her on it, then they simply couldn't be together.

~

Ari lay awake staring at the ceiling of his apartment, his thoughts swirling like a fog on the Sacramento River. It'd been three weeks since his accident, and he'd like to think it was the lack of exercise from his injured leg that was keeping him awake, but his heart told him something different.

Grace's head was on his shoulder, and her hand rested palm down on his chest, the pads of her fingers imprinted on his skin. Her soft, sleeping breaths came at regular intervals against his cheek, and as each one hit him, a new sense of indecision burned.

They'd had fun the last few weeks, no one could argue that. There'd been family dinners and movies, days lying around talking, and it'd been nice to have some time off work while his leg had been healing. He and Grace had become closer. But as his leg improved, and he began to think about getting back to his life in the city, something ate away at him. It was clear what she wanted from him—she hadn't hidden it and made no excuses for it—a life of certainty and stability. She wanted the white dress and the flower girls and a mortgage to chain them together for the next few decades. She wanted to be Mr. and Mrs., a two-headed being that would walk the earth from their wedding day onward, retreating from their real selves and the individual dreams they'd once had.

He loved her. He was certain of it. Only because he'd never had this overwhelming, heart-hurting ache whenever he thought of being away from her. Every time he closed his eyes, it was the deep blue of her own that filled his vision. It was her laugh that kept ringing in his ears, long after she'd gone to sleep, that was his downfall. Her confidence and charisma, her sense of fun, and her ability to bring happiness to other people—those were the things he wanted to experience every day, but not within the confines of marriage

But, in all of this, there was one truth he couldn't ignore. Marriages damaged people. Every minute of every day he was on the job proved that fact. They brought nobody happiness. And it wasn't only his work that made him believe this. It was his own parents. He saw what was happening to them and to Lane, who had sacrificed so many of his own dreams for Yasmin.

Maybe if Grace wasn't in the business of weddings it wouldn't be such an insurmountable issue, but she saw the act of bringing two people together as far more than a job. For Grace, as it had been to his parents when they were younger, it was a vocation, something that brought her own life personal joy and meaning. Her whole reason for being on Earth was to help a couple realize that final act of commitment, and he completely understood that she didn't want to be a walking advertisement for divorce.

Tension built in his body as each new thought formed in his head. Grace must have sensed it, too, because she stirred and muttered something in her sleep.

*Riding my bike will help this feeling go away.*

Accelerating along a highway, the wind sliding across his body so every cell came alive, was the only thing that would always give him peace. The guy at the shop had called last night and said his bike was finally ready, so he may as well go get it now.

Gently, he lifted Grace's hand and lay it on the coverlet. Brushing back a strand of her hair, he kissed her gently on the cheek and then eased himself out of bed. He'd only be gone an hour, two at most—get an Uber to the shop and ride back—but he knew in his soul that when he returned, he'd have the answer.

He moved quietly, pulling the covers over Grace and stepping softly away. Dragging on his jeans, he winced a little as he twisted his injured leg. Quickly, he threw on the T-shirt he'd worn last night and turned to leave the room.

He was almost at the door when Grace stirred.

"Hey, mister."

He turned back to see the light from the sun through the window had lit her up like an angel in soft focus, and he stood still, captured as always by her beauty.

She brushed back her hair and squinted at him. "What time is it?" Her voice was a sexy whisper. "Where are you going all dressed up like that?"

He moved back to the bed and sat down.

"Are you okay?" she asked. "Is your leg bothering you?"

He took her hand in his and squeezed it. "Go back to sleep, beautiful. I'm going to pick up my bike and go for a quick ride. I'll only be an hour or so, and when I get back I'll wake you up with a coffee."

Now she was fully awake. She hoisted herself up the bed until she was sitting. She attempted to pull the sheet up, but her honeyed skin was exposed.

"Really? You can't walk down the stairs comfortably, let alone ride a bike. And have you forgotten that it was the bike that caused the problem in the first place?"

The muscles in his jaw tensed as he tried to smile without letting her know what he really felt. "You know it wasn't the bike—it was the other guy who ran a red light."

"But it's so unsafe," she said. "Maybe the bike shop could

drop it back." She wriggled closer to him. "Or I could drive you over there." Her tone had become more definite.

He blinked. This was it. This was what had been gnawing away at him in the last few weeks. He hadn't expected it to come quite so soon—only if they were married—but here it was, staring him right in the face.

Her hand was wooden in his grasp. "I'm sorry it's not what you want, but I need my bike. It's a huge part of my life, and while I understand that it scares you, it's important to me."

Her face dropped. "So, you'll leave me here, waiting and worrying that I'm going to be called out to another accident? Doesn't that strike you as selfish?"

He stood, knowing he should say nothing but determined she should know how he really felt. "And don't you think what you are asking is selfish? Expecting me to change something I love because it makes you uncomfortable?"

She reeled back as if he'd struck her. "Have you never worried about someone?"

"Of course, I have," he said, aware of his cooling tone but unable to stop it. "But if I really understood someone, I would know where to draw the line—when what I asked would be too much for them, and our relationship, to bear." He turned to leave.

"This is not how relationships work, Ari."

He froze, his back to her

"When you're with someone, you consider their feelings as well as your own. And when you care deeply about someone, you hope with all your heart that they care enough to respect your wishes."

"But it doesn't feel like you're doing that," he said.

The sound of her sucking in a breath almost made him turn around, but there would be no winner in this.

"I know what you're thinking," she said. "You're telling

yourself that I'm trying to change you, ruin your life, just like in all of those dysfunctional relationships you deal with every day. But it's not like that. Are you so selfish you would do something that you know would make me upset?"

He swung around. "And would you deny me the one thing that's made me feel grounded since I was a teenager? Would you ask me to change that part of myself, deny that part of myself, just because it makes *you* feel better?"

Silence filled his ears as he watched her face. When she spoke, her voice was hardly above a whisper. "If you love me, yes. You'd at least consider it."

That was all she said, and no more explanation was needed. In her eyes, he could see nothing but disappointment and sadness, and it cut him to his core.

"Just go," she said, sliding back down so that the covers reached her chin.

He stayed still, knowing that whatever he did now would define their relationship forever.

Grace held her breath, willing Ari to take a step toward her. She'd been wanting to tell him what lay in the deepest part of her heart for a long time, and maybe, if she spoke now, it would make sense to him. They'd talked about this the night after the rehearsal dinner, being honest and open, not holding back. He'd said to her then that he regretted his family hadn't been like that until recently, so she knew honesty was important to him.

His face gave away the battle clearly raging within him. He wanted to go, but it was obvious her words had affected him deeply.

"Will you sit for a moment?" she asked.

For a long time, he didn't move, but finally he sat on the bed, his hands in his lap.

She rolled the corner of the coverlet between her fingers as she pushed strength into her voice. "Ari, the reason I don't want you to risk your life is because I'm in love with you." He didn't flinch. Didn't move closer.

"No," she said, not caring if this was the right time. "Not

just in love with you, but at a point where I can't imagine my life without you." His gaze searched her face, and she leaned forward to grab his hand. "I'm not asking you to stop riding your bike because I want to change you. I'm asking you to do it so that my dream of a future together doesn't end on the freeway one morning. And who would be my driving mentor then?" she joked.

A corner of his mouth lifted in the smallest of smiles, and her heart squeezed. She'd reached him. Even though he might not have said the *L* word, she could see that her concern had really touched him.

"Please come back to bed," she said, tugging at his fingers. "Now that we're both awake, it seems a shame not to be doing something together."

He moved closer, and still without speaking, he cupped the side of her face with his hand. When he leaned in and their lips met, his kiss was like none they'd shared before. He kissed her hungrily, as if they'd crossed some line and he could now really show her how he felt. It didn't matter that he hadn't said he loved her; she could tell by the passion and force of that kiss that what she'd said to him had stirred something inside him.

He paused for a moment and then dragged off his T-shirt. The gods on his skin sprang to life as he moved his body over hers. She slid her hands over his skin, and he moaned into her hair.

"You push me so hard," he whispered. "But no matter what, I can't get enough of you."

She held him close, wondering if she'd said too much too soon, but thankful that for now, at least, they were still together.

·  ·  ·

An hour later, Grace woke in Ari's arms, and a sense of security wrapped itself around her. She'd worn her heart on her sleeve, told Ari what some of her fears were, told him what he meant to her, and he was still here.

That's what you had to do when you felt this strongly about someone—tell the truth, don't sugar coat and act like things are fine when they're not. If she hadn't told Ari how she really felt about him, their relationship wouldn't have the chance to grow richer and stronger.

She breathed deep, let out a sigh and wiggled her toes in the warm depths of the bed, the movement enough to cause Ari to stir beside her.

He pulled her tight against his body, and when he kissed her neck, she turned to face him. "I'm sorry about earlier," she said. "But I can't tell you how good it feels, waking in your arms and knowing you're safe."

He tilted his chin and kissed her again, this time on the forehead. "Maybe I've found a new cure for my insomnia," he said with a grin. He started to say something else, but his phone began to ring.

"Mrs. Partella asking how it went last night?" Grace asked as he grabbed his phone from the nightstand and looked at the screen.

"No, Nick," he said, before swiping to connect and greeting his brother.

Ari was quiet for a moment, and Grace threaded her fingers through his free hand resting on the bedcover.

"What's the meeting about?" Ari asked as his gaze swung to Grace. "You think they've finally come to a decision about what they're going to do?"

Grace squeezed his hand. She hoped for all their sakes that Pia and Mano hadn't decided to split for good. They'd been visiting family and spending time at the Palace since they'd been back, but it made sense that some decisions would now need to be made.

"Then we all need to think about what's going to happen to the Palace. Pop will want to keep it, I'm certain. Too much of his life's blood is in that place." He seemed to be listening intently to his brother's answer. "Well, maybe Yasmin, then. She and Pop would work well together." He unlinked his fingers from Grace's and scrubbed a hand through his hair.

"Why do they want Grace to be there as well?"

Her heart squeezed. They must have decided to sell if they wanted her there. Maybe they wanted to tell her face-to-face that they wouldn't have any more work for her—not that it really mattered now that she had her own business. She was touched they wanted to include her. Maybe they even recognized that she might play an important part in their family one day.

When Ari had finished on the phone, she found she'd been right about the call.

"Mom and Dad have called a meeting at the Palace at lunchtime," he said. "They want all of us there, including you."

"Does Nick know what it's about?"

He shrugged. "His guess is the same as mine—that they're divorcing. I know Dad would never give up the Palace, so one of us will need to step in and work with him."

"Would Nick and Erin do it?"

"Nick says no," Ari said. "Erin will go back to running Patterson's, and Nick still has his job. Even though Pop's warmed to Erin now, I don't think he'd agree to such a tight merger between the Palace and Patterson's."

"Yasmin, then?"

"Nick doesn't think so." He was quiet for a moment before he blew out a breath. "I really don't know how Dad could do it on his own."

"Maybe they'd consider selling it?" she said.

"Why should my father sell?" Ari's voice was tight. "It was Mom's idea to leave. She walked away from decades of work, and Dad's done everything to win her back. No, my father has his pride. He won't ever give up the Palace, and I wouldn't want him to."

Grace tucked a piece of hair behind her ear. Ari's desire to see his father stay on at the Palace wasn't surprising, but the tone of his voice gave a clue to what his parents' breakup might mean to him deep down.

"So, why do you think they want me to be there?" she asked, wanting to change his focus.

"Probably to thank you for holding it all together while they went through their separation. You've helped build the Palace so that it can be a viable business again. I know my parents are really grateful to you for that."

He leaned down and kissed her, and she hoped with all her soul that he was wrong. It wouldn't be right for Mano and Pia to split, and although she'd understand why Mano might want to stay, it just wouldn't be the same without him and Pia together. She was glad she was still part of it, and she wondered if maybe together she and Ari could help his parents change their minds.

Ari pulled a chair out for Grace in the Palace's dining room and then joined her at the table. Nick and Erin had been here for some time, and Yasmin and Lane were coming through the door.

"Has anyone seen them?" Yasmin asked as she walked hand in hand with Lane. "We've been in the city checking out a new business opportunity, so I haven't seen either of them since the wedding."

"So, I take it you guys aren't interested in stepping in here?" Nick asked as he poured a glass of water for Erin.

"It doesn't fit with our plans," Lane said. "As much as we love this place, and although I really don't want to see your dad having to work through all this on his own, I don't think it's an option for us."

"Same here," said Erin. "My sister Kiera wants to have a bigger role at Patterson's, and as Nick and I hope to start a family soon, we don't really want to be getting into something new."

The four of them turned to him, and Ari shrugged. "No point looking at me," he said. "Mom and Dad would rather give the Palace away to charity than have me running things."

The others laughed, but beside him Grace cleared her throat. "I can't see why Ari couldn't help your dad run a place like this. He's certainly worked well with me in the past few weeks."

Yasmin and Nick began to chuckle, but a noise at the door caused them all to turn. First his mother walked into the room. She seemed years younger than when she'd told everyone she was leaving months before, and although it hurt Ari to admit it, he wouldn't want to see her go back to her tired and stressed self, no matter how much he wanted his parents to stay together.

"Hello, my darlings!" she said as she came in. Ari stood to pull a chair out for his mother, and when she lifted her cheek to him, he kissed her.

"I can't tell you how wonderful it is to see you all here," she said. "It seems like only yesterday that I was feeding Aristotle in his high chair while Nick read out the back of the cereal packet and Yasmin crawled around on the floor."

"You have a lot of memories in this place, Ma," Ari said as he reached for her water glass. "Too many to just throw away on a whim." His mother's mouth formed a straight line, and when he turned to Grace, there was a small frown on her forehead.

"*Yiasou ola!*" Mano shouted as he came in. Unusually for him, he was dressed in a formal shirt and tie, and his normally unruly hair had been groomed into a tidy style.

Momentarily, Ari wondered if they'd misunderstood the reason for this meeting. Maybe his parents were going to stay here. Why else would his father have such a beaming smile?

Instead of sitting at the head of the table as he normally did, Mano indicated to Nick that he should swap seats. When everything had been rearranged, everyone was seated but Mano. Ari's mother was seated to his father's right, and she was looking around at each of her children.

Mano nervously cleared his throat. Ari's heart went out to his father, whose hair seemed grayer than he remembered. It wasn't right that a man who had worked so hard for something all his life should be made to struggle on alone at his age.

"You will all be guessing why I have brought you here, and I thank you for taking the time." Mano's hands gripped the back of the chair, and his knuckles were white. "It is certainly a wonderful time in his life when a father can see his children all together, as well as their partners, all under the same roof."

Pia nodded and smiled, and Ari realized this could be the last time they were all in the same room together.

"Today I want to tell you that Pia and I have made a decision that is going to affect all your lives."

Ari took in the serious faces of his brother and sister and then turned back to his father.

"We have decided, after forty years, to make a change. It's a big change, and one that I hope you will support us in.

Whatever happens, I want you to know that our love for you will never cease."

Grace reached for Ari's hand and squeezed it. She, as much as anyone, would know what it meant for his father—losing his mother and having to carry on here alone.

Mano pulled a large handkerchief from his pocket and wiped it across his eyes. When he had finished, he cleared his throat and then placed his hand on Pia's shoulder.

"After much discussion, and plenty of negotiation, your mother and I have decided to put all our attention and energy into healing our marriage, and for that reason, we have decided to go back to Greece together for an indefinite period so that we can focus on each other alone. We need to be away from distractions and the wants and needs of others. For too long, we have put others before ourselves, and now we want to focus on nothing more than our marriage and our future life together."

A chorus of gasps went up from around the table, and then there was a scraping of chairs as first Yasmin, then Nick and Erin, left their seats to come and hug Mano and Pia.

Ari stayed where he was and tried to absorb the news.

"Isn't that fantastic?" Grace whispered in his ear. Her voice wobbled, and when he turned to her, she had tears brimming. "That has to be one of the most romantic things I've ever heard."

For a moment, Ari said nothing, just surveyed the scene before him and wondered if everyone had gone mad. Then he couldn't contain himself any longer.

"Are you kidding me, Dad?"

There was silence as everyone turned to him. His heart drummed deep in his chest, but he couldn't halt the tide of words that burst from him. "After forty years, you'd give up everything you've worked for because Mom gave you an ultimatum?"

Mano smiled broadly. "There was no ultimatum, son. Your mother and I have been discussing this since we came back for Nick's wedding. While we were in Greece, we realized we still had the future of the Palace hanging over us. But when we had time back here and could see the way you were all happy with your own lives, only then did we realize we needed to let this place go." He put his hand on Pia's shoulder, and she smiled up at him. "And in letting it go, we can spend time and energy on each other, which is the way it should be."

Ari addressed his mother. "Is this what you really want, Mom? You'd ask Dad to give up the most important thing to him for only *the possibility* that it might save your marriage? Even after he dropped everything and followed you to Greece?"

Pia's face had softened. "It is your father's choice, Ari. I have not made him choose me over the Palace."

"Well, I think it's wonderful," Yasmin said, glaring at Ari. "You'll certainly have the support of Lane and me."

"And we'll be sad to see the Palace go, but if that's what both of you really want," Nick added.

"Of course, it would be our greatest joy if one of you would like to take over the Palace," Mano said, "but we would also like the freedom of a nest egg while we rebuild our lives, so we think it best that we sell."

Ari shook his head, incredulous at what he was hearing. "Excuse me for a moment," he said.

He pushed his chair back, walked out of the room and into the courtyard. He wasn't surprised to hear Grace's footsteps behind him.

"Ari, what is it?" she asked as she came toward him. "Why are you so upset? You must be pleased that your parents have decided to give their marriage another shot."

He sat on a bench by Monty's cage and shook his head. "You just don't get it, do you?"

~

"What don't I get?" Dread and understanding swirled through Grace's body.

"That Dad has given up on his dream!" He swept an arm out. "Look at all of this. My father built this over years. *Decades*." He pointed to a row of trees. "I remember how he tended those stupid trees, put covers on them in winter, stood out here in the early morning and watered them. My father doesn't want to leave this place and go back to Greece with my mother, but he has no *choice*."

"Of course he has a choice," Grace said, hoping if she kept her voice low, Ari would too. "He could walk away from his marriage. He could put money and buildings and *things* before your mother, but he hasn't."

"He didn't because he *can't*," Ari said, his jaw tight. "He's lost the ability to stick up for himself, lost the ability to really know what makes him happy." He held his hands wide. "For God's sake, he doesn't even know who he is anymore."

"I don't understand why this upsets you so much," Grace said. "Your father is his own person. He's responsible for the decisions he makes in his life."

"That's where you're wrong," Ari said. "Trust me, I know what it's like for people to try and change you, try to get you to be good in school, or go to university. Sometimes those things are *impossible*."

He was making this about himself, thinking about how much he didn't like it when people tried to change him. A sneaking dread crawled through Grace's thoughts. Was this a warning for her? Was this about what had happened between them this morning?

She sat beside him on the bench and took his hand in hers. "I think what you're discounting here is that your father is doing this for love. He's putting his wants and needs aside for your mother because he loves her so deeply."

"If she loved him enough, she would *never* have asked him to do it." His tone was hard and cold, and she could sense him pulling further away from her. The worry became a tightly knotted ball in her stomach.

"Are we still talking about your parents or about you and me?"

Ari was silent for a beat, then two. He slowly turned to her. "I don't think it's real love when you try to change someone."

Her heart thudded in her throat as she tried to compose herself. "Love is all about compromise," she said tightly. "Working on new ways of doing things as a couple is part of being in a relationship."

"Compromise is about going to one person's family for Christmas one year and the other the next. It's not asking someone to give up a core part of themselves."

"That's not what I was asking you to do," she said as she bit back tears.

He touched her arm. "You deserve so much more than someone like me," he said. "Someone who can give you the wedding of your dreams. Someone who can be reliable and steady. I'm none of those things."

No, he wasn't going to do this to her. He was the one who'd spoken about people who lose themselves in relationships, and she knew from her deepest heart that wasn't what had happened to her.

"*None* of those things are reasons why we shouldn't be together," Grace said, fighting the tremor in her lip. "They're minuscule problems compared to the real reason a relationship between us would never work."

He seemed surprised for a moment, then his face softened.

"I could not *bear* to spend my life with someone who can't recognize an act of love when they see it." She pulled in a breath, shocked at her strength as she said all of this aloud. "You know what I think? I think you're just too afraid to love. You've put up walls and barriers to people since you were a teenager, and as soon as anyone gets under your skin, you head for the hills. Well, I'll tell you something, Ari Katsalos—that's not good enough for me. I want to be with a man who celebrates love and celebrates *me*. Not someone who's so insecure that he can't compromise and grow as a couple. I get that you're scared, and I understand where that comes from, but a life without the ability to love someone deeply, and to recognize when someone feels that way about you, is a life half lived."

"I can't offer you everything you want," he said flatly.

She scoffed so hard the back of her throat hurt. "You think all I want is a big white dress and 'here comes the bride'? Then that tells me how little you really know me. I don't believe in marriage because of the wedding ceremony. I believe in marriage as a partnership, a deep and trusting friendship where two people compromise. *Every. Single. Day.* Just as your mother and father are doing in that dining room right now." Touching her hand to her face, she was surprised to feel tears. She didn't want him to see her cry. Didn't want him to think that his words made her sad. They made her angry—angry that after all they'd gone through, after every secret she'd shared with him, all he could think was that she would try and change him.

She stood and brushed her damp hands against her skirt. "Please say goodbye to your family for me. I'm sad that the Palace will be sold, but I'm overjoyed that your parents are working together to find their happiness again. I hope that happens for you one day too." She turned and stumbled toward the path that led out to the road. She could hear him calling her name, and for a short time, she heard his boots hitting the pavement as he came after her. When the noise died away and she realized she was on her own, she let her tears fall in body-shaking sobs.

*A*ri parked his bike, stuck his helmet under one arm, and walked down Sixth Street, composing himself into some sense of confidence and order. It had been two weeks since Grace had walked out on him at the Palace, two weeks since his parents had dropped their bombshell on the family, and through all that time, it had been like living in an alternate reality.

One part of his brain kept telling him he'd done the right thing letting Grace go. From now on, he was free to do whatever he wanted. He could move back to the city and not always worry that he was doing something wrong. Another part of him, though, was convinced he'd made the biggest mistake of his life.

If he could've chosen anywhere to be for lunch today, it wouldn't have been with his loved-up brother and soon-to-be-married sister and their respective partners, but he owed his family after he'd made such a scene in front of his parents, and they obviously wanted to talk to him about something.

He pushed through the doors of the restaurant and

unzipped his jacket. The four of them were already there, and he waved hello. They must think him a loser, letting someone like Grace go, but he was used to them thinking he couldn't really pull things together, so at least that gave him a tick for consistency.

"Hey," he said. He kissed his sister and sister-in-law, then shook his brother's and Lane's hands.

After they made small talk and ordered lunch, it was Nick who got down to business. "So, we want to be sure that you're okay with the sale of the Palace going ahead. We've already caught up and discussed the fact that none of us want to take it over."

Ari took a French fry and bit into it. He was aware of four sets of eyes on him, and he didn't want to let it show. "If you mean, am I happy it's being sold? No." He shrugged. "If you're asking if I have a solution for keeping it… I don't have an answer to that either."

"How about Grace?" Yasmin said slowly. "Do you think she might consider buying it? Some of it, even? I've thought about giving her a call, but wanted to talk to you about that first, since things ended so badly between you. I know she wanted to branch out on her own, but having a ready-made business without all of us there to interfere…maybe she'd consider it."

Ari pushed away the sting that the sound of Grace's name had caused and looked around at each of them. "I haven't spoken to Grace. I really don't know what she wants to do."

"That's hardly a surprise," Nick said.

"What do you mean by that?" Ari asked, bristling.

His brother leaned forward and crossed his arms on the table—just like the times his parents had tried to make him stay in school and Nick had pulled rank as big brother to support them. "Anyone could see she was the best thing to happen to you in years."

Ari nodded slowly, trying to loosen the tightness in his voice. "And I needed something to happen to me, right? Because I can never quite get things right on my own."

"That's not what Nick meant," Yasmin said.

"Yes, it is," Ari said. "That's what Nick and Mom and you have always thought. If only Ari could find someone to fix him, then he'd be fine. And then I found someone and screwed it up, right?"

He mentally kicked himself. He didn't need to prove anything to his family. He'd been fine on his own for years. This is exactly what they'd expect from him, to come out fighting, and he didn't like it about himself.

Erin touched his arm. "Why would you need fixing?" she asked. "You're the one who's finally turned everything around for the Palace. Yasmin and Lane tried, Nick and I tried, but it was you and Grace who really managed to pull things off. And according to Grace, that was in large part down to your ability to get things done."

Ari turned to her. That was the nicest thing anyone had said to him...since Grace had said he made her feel alive again.

His chest tightened. God, he missed her. At times like this, he needed to remind himself that she was better off without him. She deserved to have everything she'd always dreamed of, and that wasn't a guy like him.

"You've done a huge favor for all of us," Lane said. "We were so caught up in our relationships and ready to march off into the world, but you were the one who was around the whole time. You kept checking in on us, making sure Pia and Mano were okay."

Ari looked at Lane, sitting next to his sister. He'd always been a successful guy, but he'd had a pretty hard time growing up, and since he'd been with Yasmin, he'd really embraced the idea of family. And Nick...well, who would have thought mathematical, theoretical Nick would've fallen head over heels for Erin Patterson? She'd challenged him as an equal, and she'd won their wager in the end, but it was Nick who always said he felt he'd won the lottery.

He scrubbed a hand through his hair.

"What is it, Ari?"

Yasmin had always known him the best. When she'd gotten dengue fever working in Borneo and hadn't wanted to tell their parents the full story, he'd called her often, and she'd told him how much she loved her family and how it was the thought of them all together again that had helped her to pull through.

He let out a long sigh. "I don't know. I guess I've always had this idea that marriage changes you, and I'd tried so hard to resist people changing me when I was younger that it wasn't something I wanted for myself. I thought about that happening with Grace and me, and then it was reinforced by Dad deciding to go and work on his marriage with Mom, and I...I didn't want to be changed."

"*Of course* marriage changes you" Yasmin said. "In ways you can't even imagine, things you hadn't dared hope for. Take Mom. She's gained so much inner strength through being in business with Dad."

"And look how Dad has changed being married to Mom," Nick added. "I don't ever remember him crying when we were younger, but he's taken on that real emotional response that Mom has, and he's not afraid to wear his heart on his sleeve. It feels as though every time I see him lately, he has that big old handkerchief out, and it's more often than not tears of joy."

"And Grace has changed you already," Erin said.

Everyone turned to her. Hearing Grace's name again was enough to have Ari's ears straining, desperate to talk about her.

"How do you figure that?" he asked.

Erin smiled her warm, all-encompassing smile. "You seem a lot more open about things for starters. Even this conversation we're having now. It wouldn't have happened six months ago."

Nick scoffed. "Ari's never had a problem with telling it like it is."

"But, honey, telling it like it is and telling it how you *feel* are completely different," Erin said as she turned to her husband then back to Ari. "What I'm talking about is the way you seem so much more up-front about things now. It's true we didn't know each other well before Nick and I were married, but you didn't strike me back then as someone who'd talk about the way you really feel in front of your whole family."

Nick frowned a little and nodded. Erin was certainly the first person Ari could remember who could put Nick in his place.

"Erin's right," Yasmin said. "You've got to admit that you've always carried a bit of a chip on your shoulder, but in the last few weeks you've shown a completely different side of yourself."

He thought of the casual way Grace had shown him how to get text read back to him, the fact she'd told him he wasn't really special after all, that everyone had something they could hide behind. Then there was the audio book she'd downloaded for him on the history of Harley-Davidsons— the first book he'd attempted to read in years. Erin was right, Grace had already changed him, and the changes were things he kind of liked about himself now.

"So, how do you know when you've met *the one*?" Ari asked, looking around the table. "How do you know when someone's worth changing for? And what happens when you make all of these changes and it doesn't work out?"

"That's easy," Lane said as he turned to Yasmin. "When you look in the mirror and see a better version of yourself reflected back, and you know deep down that this one person has found that person—the *real* you—then you know it's always going to be worth it."

Ari's throat tightened. *The Stranger* song he'd told Grace about—he'd thought it was all about waking up and finding yourself next to a person you didn't know. Could it be that Grace had helped Ari find the real version of himself? His brother and sister and their partners certainly seemed to think they were seeing a whole new side of him.

"What if it's too late?" he said to himself, the table, and anyone else who might be listening.

"If it's true love, it's never too late," Yasmin said. "That's the thing you didn't understand about Mom and Dad. They can see their love is ever-changing, and they've decided to hang onto each other, even when those changes have been difficult."

"Because for Mom," Nick said, "it wasn't Dad that was the issue, it was the business and the fact the Palace was pulling them away from each other. Once they agreed to be finished with the Palace, then they could truly concentrate on each other."

Erin reached over and laid a hand on his arm. "You know what you need to do," she said. "Nothing we tell you will change anything."

As her working day came to an end, Grace balanced a coffee and a donut in one hand and took the pile of mail Lettie had given her with the other.

"You go home," she said to her friend. "I'll finish up here." They'd had an incredibly busy day, and all Grace wanted to do was get on top of things while the store was quiet and she was alone. As she'd done most days in the last couple of weeks, she planned on staying as late as she could to avoid going home to another endless night of lying awake and thinking of Ari.

After she'd walked out on him at the Palace, she'd hurriedly packed up her things at the apartment and moved in with her brother. Finding a home of her own was on her list of things to do—maybe that would help heal the cold, empty place that was her heart without Ari.

"Don't work too late," Lettie said as she slung her bag over her shoulder. "I'm worried that right now your blood is nothing but caffeine and sugar."

Grace blew a kiss to her gorgeous, caring friend. "Just a few more emails to finish and then I'm going to work on a plan for the rose arch they want for the Lomax wedding next month."

Lettie opened her mouth to say something, then stopped. Her forehead was creased in a frown and her lips were tight.

"What's up?" Grace asked with a piece of donut in her mouth.

"You know I'm here whenever you want to talk about Ari," Lettie said slowly. "Has he phoned again?"

His name sliced through her and Grace flicked through the pile of mail, hoping the pain hadn't shown on her face. "I've missed a few calls from him, but I haven't listened to the messages."

"Maybe he's sorry," Lettie said quietly. "You seemed so into him, and if he's had some time to think about things, perhaps he wants to give things another try..."

Pretending there was a way through this was a short-lived relief, but the searing brand of reality that came afterward hurt too much for her to let it happen often. She found herself holding a brochure for limousines and remembered having a fantasy about her own wedding to Ari—a perfectly sunny day, lots of laughter and champagne, and Ari saying she made him the happiest man in the world.

*Bam.* Yes, a total fantasy.

She smiled back at Lettie, trying to force strength into her voice. "He's not going to suggest giving things another try. I'm the one who called things off, remember?"

The vision of that day played like a movie reel in her head —her world falling away from beneath her, the sound of Ari calling after her as she ran, and the voice in her head that said, '*You've let it happen again*.'

How could she get someone so wrong? So many times? At the beginning, she'd known that a guy like Ari would make her lose focus. If she'd only listened to herself, maybe then she wouldn't have fallen for him so completely, leaving her with this constant pain that wrapped around her soul.

"Doesn't mean you couldn't reconnect," Lettie said, looking at Grace from beneath her lashes. "Maybe try to work things through. He just seemed so…gorgeous."

"That's the whole problem right there. If only gorgeous was enough…"

Absently, Grace tossed the mail on the counter, and a white envelope fell out of the stack of bills. It had been so long since she'd received a personal letter that she reached for it. Maybe it was a congratulations card for the store opening.

"Do you know if he's gone back to the city yet?" Lettie asked.

Whose writing was this on the front of the envelope? It was so simple and a little unsteady. "No, I'm not sure," she said as she opened the envelope and took out a card.

"I just wonder if it's all a big misunderstanding."

She opened the card then looked back at her friend. "There was no misunderstanding, Lettie. Ari's a guy who's never going to share my belief in marriage. He's always going to think that a wedding means giving up part of yourself. That you can't love someone deeply without them changing you. He's never going to understand the risks you have to take with love. How a marriage is not about giving up who you are but about *finding* another part of yourself. I could never be with someone who didn't open themselves up to that."

Poor Lettie didn't deserve a mini sermon. She glanced down at the card, and the minute her eyes scanned the message her body froze.

*Dear Grace, I never said I loved you because I thought it meant giving up a part of myself. Now that I understand the true meaning of losing something so precious—you—I finally know what real love is. I know the stars say you and I are not a good match, but in my beating heart you will live forever. Love always, Ari.*

"Grace, what is it?"

Blood pounded hot and hard at her temples.

*His* beating heart. *Her* beating heart.

Where had she seen those words before?

*Taped to his apartment walls.*

Tears sprang to her eyes at the thought of him copying out those words…checking and double checking. "Just a message," she said. "A message I never expected to get—not like this anyway."

"Think about what I said, will you?" Lettie said as she moved toward the door. "I can't believe there's not some way you two could work things out."

Grace waved her friend goodbye, and when she was finally standing in the quiet of the empty store, she let the backed-up tears fall. There was something so deeply touching about Ari revealing a part of himself she hadn't seen before—his uncertain and carefully crafted handwriting. It made her want to shout with frustration that there were so many things she hadn't learned about him and now never would. It was too late; it was just all too late.

She plucked a tissue from a box on the counter, blew her nose, and was ready to throw the tissue and the torn envelope into the trash, when she noticed another white envelope in the pile of mail. She ripped it open and found a professionally printed invitation.

*The Aegean Palace requests the company of Grace Bennett— Wedding Planners to help celebrate our new management and a whole new world of happily-ever-afters.*

Her heart squeezed so tight, she gasped. That was a fast turnaround for Pia and Mano. Maybe Erin and Nick had decided to take things over and combine with Patterson's. Or perhaps Yasmin and Lane had bought it as part of Lane's restaurant chain. Part of her didn't know if she could face going back there—the beautiful memories of her time with Ari, the sadness of their final moments together—but another part of her knew how important the link with the Palace would be for her business. She couldn't pretend it didn't exist, and one thing she was certain of was that Ari would be miles away from there by now—he'd have gone back to his free life in the city as soon as he could.

Maybe attending this relaunch would be the perfect way for her to move on as well.

Ari sat at a table in the dining room of the Palace and drummed his fingers on the table, before standing up, pushing the chair in, and leaning against it.

No, that didn't feel right either. He pulled the chair out and sat again, this time making sure the cutlery on the white table cloth was straight.

He thought back to all the times he'd driven his bike up here from the city. How he'd counted down the days until he could leave again, get back to freedom and no responsibility.

It was a lifetime ago.

Polly's voice drifted in from the front gate, where she was welcoming people, and his parents would be down soon. He breathed in, then out, and tried running over the speech in his head one more time.

Boris wove in and out of his legs under the table, and he absently bent down and scratched the old boy's cheek.

"What do you think, Boris? Mara will be moving into her new place soon, so you won't have to put up with Monty's abuse much longer." The vibration of the cat's purr pulsed through his fingers and steadied his racing mind for a moment. He was about to take one of the biggest risks of his life and had no idea if he'd be able to pull it off.

He knew Grace would be here to witness it because he'd asked Polly to call and check, using the excuse that she needed numbers for catering. Not even Polly knew what today was about, so she couldn't have let anything slip. He brushed his clammy palms up and down on his trousers and stood again.

The gate to the courtyard opened, and he pushed his chair in and moved outside. Boris got up from where he'd just settled himself in the sun on the dining room floor and followed him out the door. Ari's chest squeezed tight like a vice.

When Nick and Erin moved toward him, he let out a quiet sigh. Too much more of this and he was going to end up a quaking mess in the corner.

"Hey, little bro," Nick said as he walked hand in hand with Erin. "Do you know what all this is about?"

Ari shrugged. "I guess what the invitation said." He hoped his face wasn't showing the storm of emotion whipping through his body. "Always an excuse for a good time at the Palace."

"Well, your mom and dad must know," Erin said, before she kissed Ari on the cheek. "Aren't they going back to Greece later tonight?"

"That's the plan." Ari stole a glance at the courtyard gate, but no one else came through.

"They must've had plenty of ready cash, these new buyers," Nick said as he went behind the outdoor bar and pulled out a bottle of wine and a glass before he stopped still. "Actually, is it okay if I get a drink, or do we need to pay now?"

Ari cleared his throat. "I'm pretty sure the changeover's not complete until tomorrow, so you're good."

"Well, I'm so pleased for your parents," Erin said as she pushed her long blonde hair over her shoulder. "They must feel so free knowing they can go back to Greece and just focus on each other. I hope they come back often though. You know Yasmin messaged us this morning and asked if it was us that had bought the Palace." Erin took the glass of wine Nick offered. "But maybe that was a ruse. What do you think, Ari? Could Yasmin and Lane have bought the Palace from your parents?"

"Mom!" Ari called to his mother who had just entered the courtyard a few steps in front of his father, thankful for the interruption.

Pia waited until Mano caught her up and then linked her arm in his before they walked across to meet them all. She was wearing a bright, flowery dress and her eyes sparkled.

They stopped at Monty's cage, and Nick turned to Ari. "Don't tell me they've sold Monty to the new owners. He's been with us since I was a teenager."

Ari moved behind the bar as his mother and father approached. He should have thought about Monty. But everything would be revealed soon anyway. "I'm pretty sure Monty won't be going anywhere. A drink, Mom? Dad?"

"The best champagne you have," Mano said as he leaned in and kissed his wife's cheek.

"You certainly seem happy," Nick said to his dad. "I guess you guys got a good settlement."

"Perfect!" Mano said as he kissed his fingers and threw his arm into the air. "It couldn't have been a better outcome, and now your beautiful mother and I can rest easy under the orange trees in Lesvos. As soon as we get there I'm going to buy a *papaki* and put your mother on the back and drive into the hills."

Pia slapped him playfully. "You are not Ari on a motorbike, Manoli. We will buy a car and drive into the hills like the old people we are."

"Won't stop us getting up to the same sort of mischief," Mano said and then ducked out of her way.

"Let's go into the restaurant," Ari said, anxious to get them inside before his parents went completely off script.

"We're here!" Yasmin called from the courtyard gate. She must've been to the salon, because her hair was even more brilliantly purple than usual. Her bottom lip trembled as she looked around her. "I can't quite believe this is the last time we'll all be here together."

"Yasmin—*koritsi-mou!*" Mano exclaimed. "There is no need for the crying. Tears of happiness are the only ones that are allowed here today. And the Palace will always be here. Your Uncle Leo and I practically built this place with our bare hands. Nothing's going to knock it down."

Lane pulled Yasmin close to him, and she brushed the back of her hand across her eyes. "I just never thought I'd have to say goodbye to this place," she said, her voice wobbling. "I can see every bead of sweat you put into painting that office wall, Dad, every piece of almond meal

Mom put into the *kourabiedes* that we ate out here when we were kids."

"Everything changes, my darling," Pia said as she came toward the assembled group. "And this is just bricks and mortar, just walls and corners. What really matters is what we build in here," she said as she placed her hand over her heart.

"Time we went inside," Ari said again, his mouth dry.

Nick lowered his voice. "I'm not sure these new owners have gotten off to a great start if they can't even be at their own party on time."

The gate to the courtyard opened, and everyone turned to see who was coming through.

*G*race pushed open the courtyard gate to the Aegean Palace and took a deep breath. There were only a few cars in the parking lot, so this obviously wasn't a big party. She'd say hello, offer her congratulations to the new owners, and then excuse herself. Early afternoon was a strange time for a party, but it did mean she could offer the excuse of work when she left early.

In theory, she should be excited to introduce herself to whomever had bought the Palace. As a newly independent wedding planner in this county, she needed to have good relationships with all the venues, but somehow, she couldn't imagine working here without the Katsalos family. She could hear the excited chatter of a group close to the main building and wondered who was here. She'd recognized Lane's Mercedes in the parking lot, so did that mean he and Yasmin had bought the Palace? Or just that they'd been invited too? Ari's bike was nowhere to be seen, which created a complicated ball of relief and sadness inside her.

When she pushed the gate shut, she was delighted to see Mano and Pia walking toward her.

"Oh, I thought you'd gone!" she exclaimed as tears stung the back of her nose. "I'm so glad I can say goodbye."

"It will never be goodbye for us," Mano said in his booming voice. "You will come to see us in Greece, Grace. You can come and witness how we celebrate weddings on the island, and I can show you the little church where Pia and I were married. And besides that, we have so many excuses to come back here and visit." His eyes twinkled.

She gave him a hug and then Pia, but when she looked over the older woman's shoulder, she froze. Ari was walking toward her.

Pia and Mano melted away and all she could focus on was Ari's gaze burning into her.

"Hey, Grace," he said in that deeply soothing voice. Only she wasn't soothed, she was panicked and red-faced and didn't know what to do next. Why had she been so sure he wouldn't be here? But he probably felt the same way she did. How on Earth was she going to get through the next hour or so without falling to pieces?

"We'll see you two inside," Pia said, and Ari kissed his mother before drawing closer to Grace. She was vaguely aware of the group moving into the restaurant, and her cheeks burned at the thought of being left alone with this man and trying to pretend that he hadn't broken her heart.

"How are you?" he said. "I hope you don't feel ambushed."

She held her hands in front of her, knitting her fingers together and trying not to show the wellspring of sadness that threatened to erupt from inside. "Why should I feel ambushed?" she asked. "I presume you're here to congratulate the new owners, too, and why wouldn't you, when this place has played such an important part in your life." She hated that she sounded so formal, but wasn't this the kind of relationship he wanted with her now?

He nodded. "Before we go inside, I want to tell you how

sorry I am for what happened the last time we were here together."

"Thank you," she said. "I was grateful for the note you wrote saying the same thing." Her fingers were clammy so she brushed them on the sides of her skirt. "You were being honest when you said what you did that day, and I appreciated that. I just wish we'd put a stop to it much earlier so that—"

She cleared her throat. She *would not* cry. Not because of the way his eyes had softened when she'd started to speak, not because of the achingly beautiful smile he gave her when she started to choke up, and not for the absolute, heart-wrenching sadness that was soaking her body. Where had it all gone wrong with him? Why hadn't she learned her lesson and not been blinded by her physical attraction to someone?

He took a step closer, and her heart rate hiked, just as it had always done when she was near him. Images of him making love to her, holding himself over her and whispering her name, burned like a brand on her brain and adrenaline began to wash through her as a fight or fight reflex kicked in.

"I understand why you didn't return my calls," he said quietly. "And I want you to know that when I realized the enormity of what I'd done, I spent the last week apologizing to my family. And now—"

"You don't need to apologize to me," she said, desperate for this heartbreaking, gut-wrenching meeting to be over. "You never hid what you wanted from me—a bit of fun and nothing more. I was the one who changed the rules. I was the one who went against everything I'd promised myself."

"Oh, Grace," he said. "The nights I've lain awake, wishing my reaction had been different that day, but the point is that I hadn't come to the realization that I've come to now."

She rubbed her throat. "What's that?"

"That I'm nothing without you."

Blood stilled in her veins.

"Grace," he said with the softest of smiles. "You've helped me to find myself. My *real* self. The biggest parts of me, that I'd pushed down and suppressed for so long, you encouraged me to face and accept. It's time I took some risks and stopped making excuses."

She swallowed past the lump in her throat. "That's beautiful, Ari. It really is. And most girls would be happy to be here, hearing you say that, but it doesn't change that I have a dream I can never give up on."

"I know that," he said.

"I'm so sorry to interrupt!" Pia looked sheepish as she called from the restaurant door. "Mano and I have to leave for the airport in an hour. Is it okay if we get things underway?"

"Maybe I should go," Grace said, her voice catching as she took a step back. "You'll be wanting to be with your family at a time like this." How could he do and say this now? She didn't want to be here, and most of all, she didn't want his family to see her devastation all over again.

Ari held an arm wide and gestured toward the restaurant. His gaze was fixed firmly on her face. "Grace, please come inside with me. There's something I need to explain."

She hesitated for a second, until something in his eyes, something certain and strong, made her take a step forward and follow him inside.

When she moved through the doors, her hand went to her throat as she realized it was only his family who were there. Erin and Nick stood to the left, both with smiles, but a perplexed look as well. Yasmin, her face damp with tears, was trying to smile and was being comforted by Lane. And Mano and Pia stood in the center of the group beaming like they'd won the lottery.

"Oh, Grace!" Yasmin squealed. "It *is* you. I was so hoping

things would turn out like this. I was just saying to Lane that he and I could never have achieved what we did here without you, and I know Nick and Erin feel the same, don't you guys?"

Hot, cold, clammy—her body was a mess of confusion as her eyes widened and she looked around everybody. What did Yasmin mean?

"Yasmin, I'm sorry. I don't know what you mean."

Why was she here? She wasn't part of this family, and she'd resigned her job two weeks ago. Whomever had bought the Palace had completely misjudged how happy she would be to attend this celebration.

Yasmin began to speak again, but Ari stepped into the middle of the room and held his hand up until there was silence.

"Thanks for coming, everyone."

"Wait," Nick said. "The invitation was from you?"

Ari stood straighter and seemed to take a deeper breath. "I've asked you here today to help me celebrate as the new owner of the Palace." Then he turned so he was only facing Grace, and a warm glow swept across her skin. "But before we do that, there's something else I need to say." He cleared his throat, and Nick and Yasmin exchanged glances. Neither of them seemed to know what was going on.

"Growing up, I took a lot of things for granted," Ari said, hands in his pockets. He looked first at Grace, then at his parents, and occasionally up at the ceiling. "I just expected that Mom and Dad would always be here if I needed them, that my brother and sister would put up with me, and I believed that at all costs I had to fight to remain true to myself. I didn't fit a mold that I'd believed was predetermined for me." Mano nodded enthusiastically.

"But in the last few weeks," Ari continued, "I've realized that taking things for granted is careless, and it doesn't fit with the man I want to be." He clasped his hands in front of himself.

This would be so hard for him, laying himself bare to his family. She ached to reach out and hold him, help him through this, but he was doing fine on his own.

"Through much of my life I've needed to keep people at a distance, and I'd become pretty cynical and negative. That was until I reconnected with my beautiful Grace."

Grace held her palm to her chest, mesmerized by the look in his eyes and the intimate way he addressed her.

"It was Grace who taught me that the best part of a relationship is when you learn to open yourself to finding out who you really are. Being with Grace has given me the courage to stop making excuses. Not only has she made me question my beliefs about myself and the world around me, but she's changed the way I think about love and commitment."

She brushed her fingers across her damp cheeks, overwhelmed by this beautiful man standing in front of his family and her, allowing himself to be vulnerable and open. Hope, fresh and new, flared in her chest, but she was too lost in her focus on Ari, to give it thought.

"If there's one thing being in this family has taught me, it's that you must never take anyone for granted." He turned toward his parents and smiled broadly. "Mom and Dad, I wish you the very best in your new adventures. Thanks to Grace, I now understand not only what real commitment means, but also the power it has to transform individuals and those around them. And from now on I'm committing myself to being the best son I can be." He moved to kiss his mother and his father on both cheeks, before moving back into the middle of the room.

The bubble of hope grew deeper inside Grace's heart. She'd never heard him speak like this, never *hoped* she'd hear such open and humble words from someone who'd been so closed and confident.

"And to my tenacious sister and my enigmatic brother—I had to Google those words," he said as his brother and sister both laughed loudly. "I want you to know that you've inspired me in the way you've fought for love in your life, and I've never been prouder of both of you." Yasmin rushed forward and pulled her brother into a tight hug, then Nick moved closer and slapped his brother on the back.

When they'd moved away, Ari turned to Grace and the room fell silent. "I'd have realized none of that without you in my life, Grace. Being with you has taught me to be proud of who I truly am, and not only to accept change in my life, but to embrace it. Not so long ago, you said to me that you believed in weddings because you knew that in marriage, the lives of those two would be stronger, deeper, and more magnificent because they'd made a public declaration to the people who are the most dear to them."

Her bottom lip trembled and she lost herself in his eyes as he continued. "Grace, you've taught me to *want* to be a better brother, a better son…and, I'm hoping, a good husband." Ari moved forward, took her hand in his, and then dropped to one knee. "Grace Bennett, will you make me the happiest man in the world by agreeing to be my wife?"

With one hand in Ari's and the other covering her lips, Grace had to steady herself. Was this the same man who'd let her go two weeks ago? The same man who'd sworn off marriage for good?

She knew enough about this man, his integrity and fierce loyalty, to know the real answer. In his open face and warm eyes, there was sincerity and love. If there was one thing she'd known about Ari from the very first time she'd seen him, it was that he was honest and true, and for that reason she pulled him up to stand beside her.

"Ari Katsalos," she said, "being with you, growing old with you, and being the best people we can be together would be the greatest joy of my life."

As the room erupted into shouts and tears and clapping, Grace let herself melt into Ari's hug. He kissed her long and slow, and in the very deepest part of her, she knew this was right. When they finally pulled apart, Ari held her hand in his, and together they turned to face his family.

"Being part of a family who celebrates love and commitment is something I've also taken for granted, but not any longer. Grace has made me the happiest man in the world, and as we go forward, I hope she's going to help me in my newest venture." He turned back to face Grace, and Erin and Yasmin let out a combined shriek. "Grace, if you agree, you and I will be the new owners of the Aegean Palace, and for another generation at least, we'll celebrate love and marriage right where it all began."

"Can you see anyone waiting for us?" Ari asked Grace as they moved through the airport arrivals gate. He scanned the small crowd of eager faces as people welcomed others off the plane, then reached for Grace's hand and squeezed it. It had been a grueling trip from the States to Greece, but the swell of pride that he was arriving here with her as his fiancée gave him all the energy he needed.

He leaned in until his lips touched her hair, and breathed in her scent of shampoo and sunshine, and…Grace. "Know how much I love you?" he whispered as she stopped and turned to him, a smile lighting her face.

She grinned. "Enough to close the Palace for a week and take me to a Greek island to celebrate our engagement?"

He tilted her chin so their lips were closer. "So much more." He kissed her long and slow, and when he reluctantly ended the kiss, looked around again. "I guess they're all lazing under orange trees or at the beach already. We can just get an Uber."

"Is that Costa over there by the door?"

"Yeah, it is." Ari lifted his hand and waved as Costa came towards them grinning.

"Welcome to Mytilene," his cousin said, casting an arm wide before he hugged him and kissed Grace on both cheeks. "I apologize that it's me who's picking you up. The others weren't quite ready, so I said I'd meet you."

"Ready for what?" Ari followed Costa toward the luggage carousel.

"Your parents have summoned everyone to the taverna at the top of the hill at noon, so they've asked me to take you straight there."

"A family get-together so soon? And aren't Yasmin and Lane heading off to Egypt today?"

"Yes, but the ship doesn't sail until tonight, so I guess this is the only chance for us to all be together. Even my father's coming."

"Oh, great. I haven't seen Uncle Yiannis for years. But a taverna? It's only eleven," Ari said. "You know I'm happy to eat souvlaki any day of the week, but that's pretty early."

Costa shrugged. "That's all I know. Are you guys okay to go straight there? It'll only take us about thirty minutes."

"Grace?"

"Absolutely. I can't wait to see everyone again, and a taverna sounds lovely."

They picked up their luggage and made their way into the brilliant Mediterranean sunshine, then over to Costa's car. A small group was forming nearby and a couple of people were talking behind their hands.

Grace got in, and Ari and Costa began transferring the luggage to the trunk.

"I guess you have a driver for this sort of thing in Switzerland," Ari said, grinning. "Not so easy to avoid your fan club here." He nodded toward the crowd of mainly women.

Costa chuckled as he unhooked his sunglasses from his shirt and put them on. "I hoped driving Dad's car would help with anonymity but apparently not."

"I thought you didn't come back to the island anymore," Ari said as he passed him the last bag. His cousin ran a multinational business from Geneva and was hugely wealthy. He often appeared in the society columns of fashion magazines, and he'd had a string of famous girlfriends.

"I've come back for a few weeks to fulfil a promise I made to a friend who passed away earlier this year. If it wasn't for that, I'd much prefer to be back at home and working. Okay, that's everything. Let's go."

Thirty minutes later, after a long and winding drive past silver olive trees and tiny villages, they pulled up in a taverna parking lot.

"Oh, there they all are," Grace said as Nick and Erin, Yasmin and Lane, and Alex and Mara came into view.

They got out and the others made their way over.

"Hey, little bro!" Nick said and hugged Ari. Grace kissed his sister Yasmin and her fiancé, Lane.

"Where are Mom and Dad?" Ari asked, looking around. "And Erin's not here either."

"Sorry we didn't make it to the airport," Yasmin was saying to Grace as they walked toward steps cut into the side of a hill. "We had a pretty big night at a taverna last night." She turned to Ari and grinned. "Lane and I have decided to get married here next summer, so all the aunties were wanting their say on where and when."

"Oh, that's fantastic!" Grace cried as she hugged Yasmin again.

"Yep, you'll all have to come back again for that. Of course, we thought long and hard about the Palace, but you know me, happy to do things on a whim." Yasmin linked her arm with Lane's. "We're going to Egypt later today, so I guess that's why Mom and Dad wanted us all to meet here for lunch."

"And Erin?" Ari asked again.

Nick's mouth tilted in a broad grin. "Let's just say it's morning, and she's not feeling so well. She went for a walk to clear her head, but she said she'd meet us here."

"Oh wow, Nick! Congratulations!" Ari pulled his brother into a tight hug. In only a few months, he'd found the love of his life, a whole new direction for his career, and now he'd have the honor of being an uncle. "You've told Mom and Dad?" he asked, his hand still on his brother's shoulder.

"Yeah." Nick grinned. "Mom cried for the rest of the night, and Dad spent a few hundred euros buying ouzo for everyone at the taverna."

Everyone began to climb the steps and Grace snuggled into Ari's side "Oh my goodness," she said as she looked out over the ocean. "This place is *so* beautiful. When was the last time you were here?"

"I think I was about six," Ari said as they walked hand in hand to the cliff's edge. "The things I remember most are helping my papou dig his vegetable garden and the sounds of the doves as I drifted off to sleep for my afternoon siesta. I can't wait to show you around all the little villages. We can hire a motorbike and spend whole days exploring."

Grace tilted her chin and looked up into his face. "You never came here again?"

He frowned and took a deep breath of the salty, earthy air. "The rest of my family did, when I was a teenager, but I guess I was too tied up in my own head to think any of this was important."

"And now?" she asked, a broad smile lighting her face.

He nodded. "Now it feels like anywhere I am with you will be as magic and special as this." He bent his head and kissed her again, willing this moment to go on forever.

"Are you coming?" Yasmin called from the top of a rise alongside the taverna. "You're not going to believe this."

They made their way to the brow of the small hill, and when they joined the others, they looked down into an amphitheater below.

Standing under an archway of flowers, Mano and Pia were beaming up at them.

"What in the name of—" Nick turned to look at the others.

Erin was walking toward them. "Sorry, Nick. Your mom asked me to help arrange this, and I could hardly say no."

Nick took his wife by the hand. "Trust the old man to upstage every wedding any of us has ever been involved in."

As Nick and Erin made their way hand in hand to where Mano and Pia were standing, a priest in his golden robes joined the small group below.

"Renewing their vows?" Yasmin breathed. "And they always said I was the radical one! I'm not sure where they found a Greek priest to agree to doing this outside a church, but we'd better get down there before he changes his mind."

When it was just the two of them standing on the lip of the amphitheater, Ari turned to Grace and grinned. "This is all down to you, Grace Bennett."

She turned to face him, her blonde hair blown back by the warm morning breeze, her dusky-pink lips parted in a smile.

"How on Earth is it all down to me?" she asked, laughing. "I've never even been here before."

Ari cupped her face in his hands. "Through the toughest of times, you've been there for my family. The only reason my dad could leave to support my mother was because he trusted you to take care of things. And then, when both Yasmin and Nick took over, it was you who kept things consistent and helped everyone navigate their own challenges."

Grace smiled up at him, her soft skin glowing in the sunlight.

"And now we get to support my parents renewing their vows under a beautiful Greek sky, a place where their dreams first began, and it couldn't be more perfect."

Grace linked her fingers through his and reached up on tiptoe to place the most sensual kiss on his lips. "You know how you make me feel, Ari Katsalos? Standing on this sacred place with people that you love?"

He dipped his head so their mouths were inches apart.

"Like a princess, in my own Aegean Palace. And the best part is that it isn't all a fairy tale." She breathed deep, then let it out slowly. "It's my own personal happily ever after."

Ari kissed her perfect, smiling mouth. "Let's go and witness another."

Read the next book in the **Tall, Dark and Driven** series!

*A Home for Summer* is Costa's story.

Read an excerpt from *A Home for Summer* on the following pages.

Buy *A Home for Summer* from your local book store, Amazon, or ask for it at your local library.

If you've enjoyed **Reining in the Rebel,** it would mean the world to me if you could leave me a review.

Reviews help enormously to bring my books to the attention of other readers who may enjoy them.

To leave a review, please search **Reining in the Rebel** on Amazon.com .

Thank you!!

Throughout my career, my readers have been such a key part of my writing life, and I love to keep them up-to-date with what I'm doing. I occasionally send out newsletters with details on both new releases and extra special offers for my books and others like mine. I promise I won't bombard you!

If you sign up to my mailing list, the first thing I'll send you is a **FREE** novella, ***Waiting on Forever***, the prequel to my ***Tall, Dark and Driven*** series.

*One last task to complete, then Alex Panos can fulfil a heart breaking promise. That is, if he can get past cute and quirky Mara Hemmingway.*

*On her own since she was sixteen, Mara won't be taken advantage of again—especially not by brooding and troubled Alex. Instead, she'll play him at his own game.*

*When their powerful attraction threatens to get in the way of both their dreams, someone will have to face a future of waiting on forever.*

You can claim your **FREE** novella by emailing barb@barbaradeleo.com !

NEXT UP IN THE TALL, DARK AND
DRIVEN SERIES…

**A Home for Summer**

*Costa's story*

*A Greek Island. A billionaire. A secret that can't be shared.*

While renovating the house her hippie mother left her on the Greek island of Lesvos, penny-pinching Summer Adams must confront much more than her lack of DIY skills.

When the mysterious Costa Nicoliedies comes to the rescue, the secrets he holds—about her mother and his hidden wealth and fame—challenge their deepening relationship.

As the atmosphere heats up, both Costa and Summer must revisit their tightly bound past that threatens to destroy their future.

You can read the first chapter of *A Home for Summer* on the next few pages.

Buy *A Home for Summer* from your local book store, amazon.com, or ask for it at your local library.

A HOME FOR SUMMER

LESVOS ISLAND, GREECE


Hot tears pricked her eyes as Summer Adams bent to pick up the tiny pink bead she'd spotted lying among a pile of stones in a corner of the tumbledown room. As she held it between her thumb and forefinger, gently blowing away a film of dust to reveal flecks of gold and silver, she gave in to the inevitable.

It was over. Finished. Her hopes of coming here, selling this wreck of a house and finally being able to buy the home of her heart in Brentwood Bay had disintegrated.

She wasn't a resident here, nor did she have enough money to renovate and sell—the laws of this village, this island, had wiped away all her hopes and dreams. As nausea curled in her belly, she thought of everyone she owed money to back home; everyone who, like her, was waiting for her to crack the golden egg she'd promised was waiting for her on an island in Greece.

*What a silly little fool.*

As she squinted at the tiny sphere in her hand, rage, sadness, and frustration mashed together deep within her. Then, screwing her eyes tight and with all her strength, she threw the wretched, hateful, heartbreaking thing as far as she could.

But the pain and the wanting, the sadness and anger it had sparked, stayed rooted inside her.

As her eyes flew open, a groan lodged in her throat. In a panic, imagining another part of her mother lost forever, she pushed up on the latch of the sagging door to the lane, desperate to get outside.

The door wouldn't budge. Of course it wouldn't. Maybe it was a sign, maybe—

"Hello?"

Lurching backwards at the shock of a voice from the window, her heart somersaulted at the sight of the face that poked through. Sleek black waves of hair framed an angular face, where large dark glasses sat on a regal nose. Skin the color of dusk covered the plane of a strong jaw and sat smooth across unforgettable cheekbones. The entire manly vision caused her breath to stall in her throat.

"Is this yours? Or someone else's unguided missile?" he said, strong and slow.

Her pulse skipped at the tone of his rich Greek accent. To have anyone walk down the lane in this tiny island village seemed enough of an event. The fact he spoke English and looked like her teenage impression of a Greek god seemed way too good to be true.

"I'm so sorry," she finally said, warmth spreading across her cheeks as she tried to still the rhythm in her chest. She dusted her hands on her denim shorts. "I was...cleaning up...it sort of...slipped."

Was he angry or amused?

The heavy set of his brow and the unforgiving line of his perfect mouth gave nothing away, so she spoke to fill the silence. "I've been here for at least an hour, and I'm sure nobody's walked past. I thought this part of the village must be deserted."

Leaning a strong, muscle-bound forearm on the wooden sill, he held the bead through the window. It sat pretty and fragile in his large hand as he spoke. "Not deserted. People are having their siesta. But not me. I was coming to see you. If you're Summer."

"Ahhh," Summer stuttered, "yes, yes it...achoooo!!" Her lungs pulled tight as she gasped for air.

"Bless you," he said, with the tiniest twitch of his mouth.

"Asthma," Summer rasped as she reached for the grey inhaler in her back pocket. After breathing the medicine long and deep into her lungs she managed, "All this...dust."

"I can see," he said. "Have you been stirring it up since yesterday?"

As he spoke, she imagined what sort of eyes were behind those glasses, eyes that might probe and explore her inner most desires, crack the shell of confidence she'd been trying to hold so carefully around herself ever since she'd arrived in this tiny old village.

"I was supposed to meet you yesterday, but was delayed, and didn't get to the island until late last night. My apologies."

"Kirieh...Nicoliedies, is it?" Summer said, her tongue tripping over the name, knowing she was murdering the Greek words. "My mother's lawyer in California said I should expect you some time yesterday." Her lips flattened. He might well be annoyed that he'd had to come looking for her, but at least she hadn't been the one who'd missed their meeting.

He transferred the bead to his left hand and held out his right. "Costa."

Placing her own hand in the broad palm offered, she

immediately felt the strength of him as a shiver swept up her arm.

He spoke as if those around him always listened, the smooth planes of his face held in a way that indicated assurance and mystery. "I'm Costa Nicoliedies."

The dark glasses unnerved her. Like a model in an ad for perfume, he exuded haughty indifference and attitude. She slid her hand from his grip, already missing its strength, and took a step back.

"Costa? Oh, I'm sorry," she said. "I must've heard your name wrong yesterday. Of course, that's one of my biggest problems in being here, I don't speak any Greek."

"It doesn't matter." There was upward movement in his lips, but not quite a smile. "I'm sure you'll get by."

"I'd invite you in..." She finally stepped forward again to take the bead. There was a moment's hesitation as her hand floated above his, and she tried desperately to control the nerve endings that were firing at random.

He didn't pass the bead to her, but held it flat in his palm. Waiting.

Like a bird collecting its prey, she plucked it away, shoved it into the pocket of her shorts, and again stepped backwards, out of the ring of confidence that surrounded him.

"I can't open the door." She looked away as she spoke, still aware of his intense gaze.

"No problem." Costa gripped the top of the window frame, his biceps stretching as he vaulted effortlessly through.

The black T-shirt he wore defined the dark brown of his skin. It must be every girl's fantasy to have a muscled Greek man leaping through her window, but Summer wasn't quite sure how she felt about someone being so...forward. Right at this moment though, he was her last hope to turn this situation around.

"I'm in now." He stretched his lithe frame, as if he'd completed the Olympic pole vault, then shot her a heart-stopping grin.

"So you are." Heat rushed to her face as his presence now dominated the small space. She reached for the jade *tiki* that lay at her throat and smoothed the cool green stone under her fingers. She was far more comfortable when people kept their distance, not so near she could feel their warmth.

Costa pulled off the glasses and carefully folded them. His striking eyes were now unveiled and the polished coal pupils drew her in—dark, mysterious eyes that could make you forget your own name.

"What can I do for you?" he asked as he looked around the tumbledown room. "This looks like quite a project."

Now she knew where that confidence began, she couldn't drag her gaze away and held the pendant tighter.

"Well," she said, bringing her attention back to her immediate problem, "I need your help to find a way around the island's laws. I have to get this place ready to sell, but the authorities won't let me."

"What do you mean?" His gaze swept around the room, before again settling on her. "I was told you needed someone to help translate while you sold this house. No one suggested it could be a problem."

"I'm not allowed to sell it." Her throat began to constrict again at the memory of the news she'd been given yesterday. "The person from the island housing authority I spoke to said that, as a foreigner, the only way I can renovate property to sell is if I can give proof of funds from a bank account in my name."

He fixed her with a stare as if to ask why on earth that would be a problem.

"If you knew me," she said, as she pulled the bead from her pocket again, "you'd understand that's about as likely as this little thing finding its way back to the string it was dropped from."

Costa crossed his arms in front and leaned back against the wall, his face creasing in confusion. "You came here expecting to renovate and sell the house without checking out the island's property laws first?" His tall frame reached most of the way up the wall.

The awful logic of his question caused her stomach to clench all over again. "I've never been here before. Had no idea what to expect. The house was left to me by my mother, so I just assumed I could come here and sell it, but when I arrived, I found it was in *this* state." She waved her arm to indicate the chaos that surrounded them. "My mom's lawyer never mentioned it might be so run down, or that selling it could be this complicated. If I'd known, maybe I wouldn't have—"

"And the immigration officials won't let you renovate or sell?" He looked down at the packed earth floor and smoothed it with an expensive looking boot. Despite his cool smiles, she felt something simmering beneath the polite façade. Maybe he didn't want to be here, didn't want to help. Not her, not now.

"No, they won't. Apparently, they've had people start to renovate and give up halfway through, leaving a bigger mess than when they started." She lifted her chin. "It's just a hideously vicious circle. I'm depending on a sale because I really need the money back home, but I can't sell because I don't have the money to renovate." Silence stretched between them until she spoke again. "What were you expecting to do here before all this?"

He looked up, his gaze more intense, reeling her in. "Your mother's lawyer was looking for someone to help with translation for sale deeds and the like. I was coming back for the summer, so I said I'd help, but I wasn't expecting this. What is it you need?"

Her pulse fluttered at the change in his eyes. What did she need? To get out of this house, this village, this country on the other side of the world. To get back so she could finally pay for the piece of land that seemed to be slipping from her grasp.

It was so *typical* of her mother, springing another surprise on her. To not even tell her before she died that there was a house in Greece, let alone that it was in this state...Even from the grave, she seemed intent on dragging Summer from one place to the next. Hurt and sorrow and cold, bald grief clung together inside her.

"I've only been on the island for two days," she said, trying to disguise the wobble in her voice. "I spent all of yesterday in a town about an hour away, only to be told in the end that even if I *did* have the money in the bank, I couldn't sell until the house was habitable and met their specifications." She felt her lungs tighten again at the thought of renovating this dust heap.

His gaze washed over her while she spoke, then he nodded. "This is the old part of the village and it comes under a presidential decree as being a traditional village of outstanding beauty. There are strict rules here on Lesvos about what you can do to the houses. My father's the mayor. He feels very strongly about such things. It's safer for the island authorities to impose those restrictions, so people can't change the whole style of the place."

She nodded as he repeated what she'd been told yester-day. And it made sense—from everyone's viewpoint but hers.

Costa's dark eyes scanned the room then landed directly back on her. "So, what's the problem? Can't you just get a loan and then renovate? Pay it back when you've got the proceeds of the sale?"

"No." Her heart squeezed tighter. "My bank and I aren't seeing eye to eye right now. A loan's impossible."

How could she get out of this mess without telling him her whole life story? She sighed. "I've got very little money and I have a bunch of debts due from trying to secure a piece of land I'm hoping to buy back home. I had to borrow money from a friend to buy the plane ticket to get here, and I only have enough left for a couple of nights' accommodation. Finding the house like this was all so...unexpected."

"I see."

But he didn't see and that was the problem. His voice had hardened and he seemed thrown by what she'd said. He stood against the wall, a picture of irritation, while her dream turned rapidly into a nightmare.

"You were told you had no other option than to prove you have money before you renovate?"

She sighed. "Absolutely none. The man yesterday said that anyone who wants to renovate in a protected village in Greece must follow very special rules, and the rules for foreigners state that they must show they can carry the renovation to completion. And for that they need money."

How she wished she could get on and do this all herself. Why couldn't her mother have had a house in Australia or England? *She* must have had money to buy this place, another gift from Summer's generous grandparents she suspected – the grandparents Summer had never met because her mother had cut all ties before Summer's birth. As usual, her mother had made the decision for her, assuming that her roaming way of life, owning nothing and staying nowhere for long, no home or family, would suit her daughter.

"Yes, the rules for foreigners are different in a case like this." His eyes narrowed a fraction and Summer thought she saw a slight nod, as if he'd been chewing her situation over and suddenly found a solution.

Was it possible he could help her? Was there a chance he could find a way to bend the rules so she could at least get the house ready to sell? Her heart quickened with the hope of it.

"So, you'd intended to stay in the house before you sold?" he finally asked.

"I was hoping to, at least until I had a buyer. I guess, I guess I was just too..." Her hands did the flapping thing that made her feel less out of control, but the treacherous burn of tears stalled her words.

Costa seemed unsettled by her sudden display of emotion and pulled his lips a little tighter. "That's a decent set of issues to deal with," he said matter-of-factly. "How bad is your asthma?"

She took a big breath in through her nose.

"Not bad. As long as I'm not stressed out and surrounded by dust all day. I was hoping," she continued, mentally crossing her fingers, "that you might be able to talk to the council for me, ask them if they'll make an exception. Explain that, although I don't have the money, I'll do the renovation any way they like. I just have to sell this place."

This was torturous, asking a complete stranger, a completely *gorgeous* stranger, for help, but she had no choice. Either she walked away now and lost all hope of paying off her debts and buying her dream home, or she could find a way to sell this house and have the life she'd always imagined, to finally have a home at last, one nobody could take from her...

His cool, searching stare pinned her again and this time she wished she'd never said anything. "But you'd still need money to renovate."

A bead of sweat tumbled down her back. She couldn't speak the language, couldn't meet the requirements to sell the house, and had absolutely no money. Her eyes darted away from the hold his stare had on her. She wanted to escape the flutter in her chest that began each time she waited for him to speak.

The effort to control her emotions saw a rogue sigh escape her lips. Why would a complete stranger care about helping her bend the rules? And the son of the mayor at that? It was clear by the way he looked at her, all cool and calm, that he wasn't going to say what she needed to hear. Closing her eyes, she sucked in a defensive breath in the second before he spoke the words that would surely end her dream.

"There's no way I can help you bend an island law," he said as he crossed his arms. "It's there for a good reason—to ensure people renovate *properly*, that the traditions and atmosphere of the village are protected. We can't have people coming in and putting up plastic fences and multicolored roofing iron. We also can't have people start something when they have no capacity to complete it. Our tradespeople need to know that they won't be left empty-handed or worse when some dreamer skips the country."

*Some dreamer.*

Is that what he thought of her? Her eyes opened, and for the first time she noticed tiny hints of grey in his otherwise jet-black hair. His tight and toned physique suggested youth, but the silvery streaks, maturity. "Then there's nothing I can do but walk away," she said, again feeling the prickle of backed-up tears. "I *have* no money. I just wanted to sell this...thing...so I could take some money back home and...start again."

Costa began to walk around the room. He was tall, but didn't hide the fact—his spine ramrod straight and his chin a fraction higher than was natural.

He stopped and slapped the palm of his hand on one wall, making her jump. "Most of it seems quite solid, apart from a few places where water's got in. That's why some of the brick and stone have crumbled away. It leaves plenty of dust, but really just needs to be re-packed and plastered. Our local tradespeople are very experienced at this sort of work."

He made it sound so simple, but she didn't think for a minute that getting rid of this mess would prove to be so easy.

"What's through here?"

Before she could answer, he moved to go through to the next room. He stopped at the door and pushed with a powerful shoulder, but it was stuck fast, leaving just enough of a gap to squeeze through.

Frowning slightly that he'd helped himself, but glad he seemed more interested, she followed. Maybe he *did* know a way around the law—why else would he still be here?

This room was similar to the first, albeit a little smaller. One window, again with no glass, looked out on an orange grove that ran down a gentle slope. A sweet tang of orange, mixed with the soft scent of packed earth, filled the room as the late afternoon sun threw spears of light down the faded walls. Dust waltzed in random shafts and in one corner, an old brick construction with an iron door in the center stood —some sort of fireplace.

Costa moved toward it, his eyes growing wider, a warm smile lighting his face. "I haven't seen one of these for *years*," he said, his hand on the brick top. His voice was suddenly lighter, excited even. "In the old days you'd have to light a fire in here to get hot water." He touched an old faucet that sat over the bath. "My grandparents had one. They used the hot water for washing clothes...or themselves."

Summer shuddered. She could just imagine her mother here in the nineties, with goodness knows how many other hippies, incense burning, wallowing about all day in the bath, and singing about peace, love and understanding.

Her dream bathroom floated through her imagination

—all white tiles and halogen lights, big fluffy towels and a healthy looking fern in the corner.

Costa turned to face her and leaned back against the fireplace as a mysterious look flitted across his face. "What if I was to say there *is* a way around this, a way for you to legally renovate and sell before you leave the country?"

Blood rushed to her core and Summer gave up a silent vote of thanks for whomever had sent her this wonderful man. "I'd say I'll do whatever it takes," she said, unable to stop the smile that began to push its way across her face. "Tell me—"

He held up a hand. "First I need to know how long you've got."

For a moment she wanted to fall into his soul-searching eyes. Shaking her head she took a step back. "What do you mean?"

"How long do you intend to stay?"

"Four weeks. That's all the time I've managed to take from work. I'd imagined I could sell this place quite quickly, in which case I could've gone home sooner..."

A sudden scuffle in the ceiling directly above made her leap back and she let out a small squeal at the thought something might fall on her.

"Looks as though *someone* likes living here," Costa said as they both looked up.

When he glanced back at her, his eyes softening, she could finally see a funny side to all this and for the first time her spine softened with the warmth of his concern.

"I'll tell you what I'll do," he said. "I'm back in the village for about four weeks too. If you agree with my plan, I think we could get this finished in a month." He tilted his chin. "I can't guarantee you're going to like my idea though."

"Even if there is a way for me to renovate legally, I don't have the *money* to do it," Summer said in desperation. Was he offering to pay for the work himself? Surely not. She'd never be beholden to someone like that.

"I can help you sort out a builder, a plasterer, and," he said, thumping the tap again, "maybe a plumber. It shouldn't take too long to make this place habitable."

She was grateful, of course she was, but it still didn't solve her two major problems: finding a way around the law and, if she managed *that*, finding money for the renovations. The thought that working every day with Costa could also be a very big problem was almost enough to make her turn and run right now.

***

"So you can pay for it," Costa said as he watched the light shine behind her eyes, "I'm sure I can help you find a job or two around the village."

As he spoke, Costa made a conscious effort to hide the panic plowing through him. He'd made a promise to ensure Summer left the island with everything she'd come for, and he sure as hell wasn't going to renege on it. But he hadn't counted on *this* set of circumstances.

And he'd promised Summer would never find out who'd really sent him here.

She wasn't what he'd expected. Stunning, yes, with luminous eyes that drew him in. But he had to ignore that fact and the stirring it caused in him right from the get go. He had a task to complete in as short a time as possible and, given the restrictions they were both under, the only solution to their problem was beginning to flash neon in his head.

Although her mother had written of a materialistic girl searching for her place in the world, Costa could see parts of her mother in her. Long blonde hair fell soft around her shoulders, whereas her mother's hair had been short and spiky. Even though he was only a boy then, he could remember the same delicate features he saw now.

Summer wore shorts, revealing perfect legs. Quite a contrast to his hippy teacher with her flowing skirts. But it was the pendant that lay on the pale skin of her throat that reminded him of something Summer's mother might've treasured.

Although they'd stayed in touch throughout the course of her illness, it had been years since he'd seen Caroline. He remembered the day when, as a boy, his whole class and most of the village had gone down to the jetty to wave her goodbye, everyone in tears. He'd never forgotten her, had always remembered what she'd taught him, and what he *owed* her. He remembered a vibrant, carefree person, certainly not someone as tightly coiled as the woman who stood in front of him now.

He didn't like secrets, but when Caroline had written and explained she didn't have long to live, he'd promised her anything—he'd always be in her debt and was prepared to do whatever she asked. Knowing her daughter would have to travel to Greece to claim the house, Caroline had asked if he'd look out for her only child, insisting Summer mustn't know about their communication and that he mustn't help her out financially. Apparently, her daughter was frighteningly independent.

He hoped it wouldn't take long, that he could leave this place—this town that seemed to close in on him—and get back to where he belonged as quickly as possible. It was vital that his time here be kept a secret, away from the prying lenses and crude questions the paparazzi would often fire at him. The villagers would hate it if the gossip-hungry hordes overran the town the way they did the last time he was here. He'd had to take a detour coming to the island yesterday when one particularly rabid journalist popped up in Athens airport.

There was one simple way around the island's rule—but he couldn't imagine she'd agree to it.

"What sort of job could I do here to raise the money?" Summer said, her small brow furrowing deeper. "I don't have a work permit to earn cash, but what if I could make something, do something in exchange?" Her eyes grew wider.

Not for the first time that day, Costa thought how unnecessarily difficult this was going to be. Caroline had insisted he mustn't give Summer money—apparently Summer finding a solution to that would be part of her journey—but it would be so much easier if he did. Her body language—the folded arms, the permanent little frown—made it clear she didn't want to be here either.

"You could teach English," he said, picking up on her idea. "Lots of people have learned English at school, but they're always looking to improve. I'm sure you could trade an hour or two for some plumbing, a conversation or two for some building. Maybe even help out at the school."

Her head tilted a little to the side and he could feel her indecision as she stuttered, "Oh, I don't think I'd be...I wouldn't know how to begin *teaching* someone."

Why was she so flustered? Her mother had been an inspirational teacher.

"I think you could," he said, fascinated by the way he could almost see the cogs working behind her luminous blue eyes. She wanted an easy way out of this, but there was no easy way out. What they'd have to do was the last thing he'd choose, but he would never go back on a promise.

"Do you think so?" For a second, calm seemed to cross her face and for the first time her gaze truly met his. Hope radiated out of their blue depths and something pulled tight in his chest.

Another scuffle in the roof.

Costa watched as her eyes moved to the ceiling in obvious dread, the milky skin of her neck stretching.

Her face was pale and without makeup. A blonde fringe fell across her forehead, making her appear younger than he guessed she was. Her lips, pressed together right now, held promises he imagined stealing if the moment were right...

When her gaze turned back to him, her teeth were gritted and she let out a sigh as she pulled the small pink bead from her pocket. "So tell me, how do we get around this rule? I'm prepared to do whatever it takes to get this place sale-able. What do I have to do to get started?"

Costa looked down at her, his pulse beginning to harden as the words fell from his mouth before he'd truly thought them through. It was crazy and it was outrageous, but it was what he had to do to honor the memory of her mother.

"There's only one way," he said, as he watched her eyes widen. "All you have to do is marry me."


sight of the face that poked through. Sleek black waves of hair framed an angular face, where large dark glasses sat on a regal nose. Skin the color of dusk covered the plane of a strong jaw and sat smooth across unforgettable cheekbones. The entire manly vision caused her breath to stall in her throat.

"Is this yours? Or someone else's unguided missile?" he said, strong and slow.

Her pulse skipped at the tone of his rich Greek accent. To have anyone walk down the lane in this tiny island village seemed enough of an event. The fact he spoke English and looked like her teenage impression of a Greek god seemed way too good to be true.

"I'm so sorry," she finally said, warmth spreading across

her cheeks as she tried to still the rhythm in her chest. She dusted her hands on her denim shorts. "I was...cleaning up...it sort of...slipped."

Was he angry or amused?

The heavy set of his brow and the unforgiving line of his perfect mouth gave nothing away, so she spoke to fill the silence. "I've been here for at least an hour, and I'm sure nobody's walked past. I thought this part of the village must be deserted."

Leaning a strong, muscle-bound forearm on the wooden sill, he held the bead through the window. It sat pretty and fragile in his large hand as he spoke. "Not deserted. People are having their siesta. But not me. I was coming to see you. If you're Summer."

"Ahhh," Summer stuttered, "yes, yes it...achoooo!!" Her lungs pulled tight as she gasped for air.

"Bless you," he said, with the tiniest twitch of his mouth.

"Asthma," Summer rasped as she reached for the grey inhaler in her back pocket. After breathing the medicine long and deep into her lungs she managed, "All this...dust."

"I can see," he said. "Have you been stirring it up since yesterday?"

As he spoke, she imagined what sort of eyes were behind those glasses, eyes that might probe and explore her inner most desires, crack the shell of confidence she'd been trying to hold so carefully around herself ever since she'd arrived in this tiny old village.

"I was supposed to meet you yesterday, but was delayed, and didn't get to the island until late last night."

"Kirieh...Nicoliedies, is it?" Summer said, her tongue tripping over the name, knowing she was murdering the Greek words. "My mother's lawyer in California said I should expect you some time yesterday." Her lips tightened. He might well be cross that he'd had to come looking for her, but at least she hadn't been the one who'd missed their meeting.

He transferred the bead to his left hand and held out his right. "Costa."

Placing her own hand in the broad palm offered, she immediately felt the strength of him as a shiver began where they joined and swept up her arm.

He spoke as if those around him always listened, the smooth planes of his face held in a way that indicated assurance and mystery. "I'm Costa Nicoliedies."

The dark glasses unnerved her. Like a model in an ad for perfume, he exuded haughty indifference and attitude. She slid her hand from his grip, already missing its strength, and took a step back.

"Costa? Oh, I'm sorry," she said. "I must've heard your name wrong yesterday. Of course, that's one of my biggest problems in being here, I don't speak any Greek."

"It doesn't matter." There was upward movement in his lips, but not quite a smile. "I'm sure you'll get by."

"I'd invite you in..." She finally stepped forward again to take the bead. There was a moment's hesitation as her hand floated above his, and she tried desperately to control the nerve endings that were firing at random.

He didn't pass the bead to her, but held it flat in his palm. Waiting.

Like a bird collecting its prey, she plucked it away, shoved it into the pocket of her shorts, and again stepped backwards, out of the ring of confidence that surrounded him.

"I can't open the door." She looked away as she spoke, still aware of his intense gaze.

"No problem." Costa gripped the top of the window frame, his biceps stretching as he vaulted effortlessly through.

The black T-shirt he wore defined the dark brown of his

skin. It must be every girl's fantasy to have a muscled Greek man leaping through her window, but Summer wasn't quite sure how she felt about someone being so...forward. Right at this moment though, he was her last hope to turn this situation around.

"I'm in now." He stretched his lithe frame, as if he'd completed the Olympic pole vault, then shot her a heart-stopping grin.

"So you are." Heat rushed to her face as his presence now dominated the small space. She reached for the jade *tiki* that lay at her throat and smoothed the cool green stone under her fingers. She was far more comfortable when people kept their distance, not so near she could feel their warmth.

Costa pulled off the glasses and carefully folded them. His striking eyes were now unveiled and the polished coal pupils drew her in—dark, mysterious eyes that could make you forget your own name.

"What can I do for you?" he asked. "This looks like quite a project."

Now she knew where that confidence began, she couldn't drag her gaze away and held the pendant tighter.

"Well," she said, bringing her attention back to her immediate problem, "I need your help to find a way around the island's laws. I have to get this place ready to sell, but the authorities won't let me."

"What do you mean?" His gaze swept around the room, before again settling on her. "I was told you needed someone to help translate while you sold this house. No one suggested it could be a problem."

"I'm not allowed to sell it." Her throat began to constrict again at the memory of the news she'd been given yesterday. "The person from the island housing authority I spoke to said that, as a foreigner, the only way I can renovate property to sell is if I can give proof of funds from a bank account in my name."

He fixed her with a stare as if to ask why on earth that would be a problem.

"If you knew me," she said, as she pulled the bead from her pocket again, "you'd understand that's about as likely as this little thing finding its way back to the string it was dropped from."

Costa crossed his arms in front and leaned back against the wall, his face creasing in confusion. "You came here expecting to renovate and sell the house without checking out the island's property laws first?" His tall frame reached most of the way up the wall.

The awful logic of his question caused her stomach to clench all over again. "I've never been here before. Had no idea what to expect. The house was left to me by my mother, so I just assumed I could come here and sell it, but when I arrived, I found it was in *this* state." She waved her arm to indicate the chaos that surrounded them. "My mom's lawyer never mentioned it might be so run down, or that selling it could be this complicated. If I'd known, maybe I wouldn't have—"

"And the immigration officials won't let you renovate or sell?" He looked down at the packed earth floor and smoothed it with an expensive looking boot. Despite his cool smiles, she felt something simmering beneath the polite façade. Maybe he didn't want to be here, didn't want to help. Not her, not now.

"No, they won't. Apparently, they've had people start to renovate and give up halfway through, leaving a bigger mess than when they started." She lifted her chin. "It's just a hideously vicious circle. I'm depending on a sale because I really need the money back home, but I can't sell because I don't have the money to renovate." Silence stretched between them until she spoke again. "What were you expecting to do here before all this?"

He looked up, his gaze more intense, reeling her in. "Your mother's lawyer was looking for someone to help with translation for sale deeds and the like. I was coming back for the summer, so I said I'd help, but I wasn't expecting this. What is it you need?"

Her pulse fluttered at the change in his eyes. What did she need? To get out of this house, this village, this country on the other side of the world. To get back so she could finally pay for the piece of land that seemed to be slipping from her grasp.

It was so *typical* of her mother, springing another surprise on her. To not even tell her before she died that there was a house in Greece, let alone that it was in this state...Even from the grave, she seemed intent on dragging Summer from one place to the next. Hurt and sorrow and cold, bald grief clung together inside her.

"I've only been on the island for two days," she said, trying to disguise the wobble in her voice. "I spent all of yesterday in a town about an hour away, only to be told in the end that even if I *did* have the money in the bank, I couldn't sell until the house was habitable and met their specifications." She felt her lungs tighten again at the thought of renovating this dustheap.

His gaze washed over her while she spoke, then he nodded. "This is the old part of the village and it comes under a presidential decree as being a traditional village of outstanding beauty. There are strict rules here on Lesvos about what you can do to the houses. My father's the mayor. He feels very strongly about such things. It's safer for the island authorities to impose those restrictions, so people can't change the whole style of the place."

She nodded as he repeated what she'd been told yesterday. And it made sense—from everyone's viewpoint but hers.

Costa's dark eyes scanned the room then landed directly back on her. "So, what's the problem? Can't you just get a loan and then renovate? Pay it back when you've got the proceeds of the sale?"

"No." Her heart squeezed tighter. "My bank and I aren't seeing eye to eye right now. A loan's impossible."

How could she get out of this mess without telling him her whole life story? She sighed. "I've got very little money and I have a bunch of debts due from a piece of land I'd hoped to buy back home. I had to borrow money from a friend to buy the plane ticket to get here, and I only have enough left for a couple of nights' accommodation. Finding the house like this was all so...unexpected."

"I see."

But he didn't see and that was the problem. His voice had hardened and he seemed thrown by what she'd said. He stood against the wall, a picture of irritation, while her dream turned rapidly into a nightmare.

"You were told you had no other option than to prove you have money before you renovate?"

She sighed. "Absolutely none. The man yesterday said that anyone who wants to renovate in a protected village in Greece must follow very special rules, and the rules for foreigners state that they must show they can carry the renovation to completion. And for that they need money."

How she wished she could get on and do this all herself. Why couldn't her mother have had a house in Australia or England? *She* must have had money to buy this place, another gift from Summer's generous grandparents she suspected – the grandparents Summer had never met because her mother had cut all ties before Summer's birth. As usual, her mother had made the decision for her, assuming that her roaming way of life, owning nothing and staying nowhere for long, no home or family, would suit her daughter.

"Yes, the rules for foreigners are different in a case like this." His eyes narrowed a fraction and Summer thought she saw a slight nod, as if he'd been chewing her situation over and suddenly found a solution.

Was it possible he could help her? Was there a chance he could find a way to bend the rules so she could at least get the house ready to sell? Her heart quickened with the hope of it.

"So, you'd intended to stay in the house before you sold?" he finally asked.

"I was hoping to, at least until I had a buyer. I've done plenty of travel before, but never overseas. I guess, I guess I was just too..." Her hands did the flapping thing that made her feel less out of control, but the treacherous burn of tears stalled her words.

Costa seemed unsettled by her sudden display of emotion and pulled his lips a little tighter. "That's a decent set of issues to deal with," he said matter-of-factly. "How bad is your asthma?"

She took a big breath in through her nose.

"Not bad. As long as I'm not stressed out and surrounded by dust all day. I was hoping," she continued, mentally crossing her fingers, "that you might be able to talk to the council for me, ask them if they'll make an exception. Explain that, although I don't have the money, I'll do the renovation any way they like. I just have to sell this place."

This was torturous, asking a complete stranger, a completely *gorgeous* stranger, for help, but she had no choice. Either she walked away now and lost all hope of paying off her debts and buying her dream home, or she could find a way to sell this house and have the life she'd always imagined, to finally have a home at last, one nobody could take from her...

His cool, searching stare pinned her again and this time she wished she'd never said anything. "But you'd still need money to renovate."

A bead of sweat tumbled down her back. She couldn't speak the language, couldn't meet the requirements to sell the house, and had absolutely no money. Her eyes darted away from the hold his stare had on her. She wanted to escape the flutter in her chest that began each time she waited for him to speak.

The effort to control her emotions saw a rogue sigh escape her lips. Why would a complete stranger care about helping her bend the rules? And the son of the mayor at that? It was clear by the way he looked at her, all cool and calm, that he wasn't going to say what she needed to hear. Closing her eyes, she sucked in a defensive breath in the second before he spoke the words that would surely end her dream.

"There's no way I can help you bend an island law," he said as he crossed his arms. "It's there for a good reason—to ensure people renovate *properly*, that the traditions and atmosphere of the village are protected. We can't have people coming in and putting up plastic fences and multicolored roofing iron. We also can't have people start something when they have no capacity to complete it. Our tradespeople need to know that they won't be left empty-handed or worse when some dreamer skips the country."

*Some dreamer.*

Is that what he thought of her? Her eyes opened, and for the first time she noticed tiny hints of grey in his otherwise jet-black hair. His tight and toned physique suggested youth, but the silvery streaks, maturity. "Then there's nothing I can do but walk away," she said, again feeling the prickle of backed-up tears. "I *have* no money. I just wanted to sell this...thing...so I could take some money back home and...start again."

Costa began to walk around the room. He was tall, but didn't hide the fact—his spine ramrod straight and his chin a fraction higher than was natural.

He stopped and slapped the palm of his hand on one wall, making her jump. "Most of it seems quite solid, apart from a few places where water's got in. That's why some of the brick and stone have crumbled away. It leaves plenty of dust, but really just needs to be re-packed and plastered. Our local tradespeople are very experienced at this sort of work."

He made it sound so simple, but she didn't think for a minute that getting rid of this mess would prove to be so easy.

"What's through here?"

Before she could answer, he moved to go through to the next room. He stopped at the door and pushed with a powerful shoulder, but it was stuck fast, leaving just enough of a gap to squeeze through.

Frowning slightly that he'd helped himself, but glad he seemed more interested, she followed. Maybe he *did* know a way around the law—why else would he still be here?

This room was similar to the first, albeit a little smaller. One window, again with no glass, looked out on an orange grove and orchard that ran down a small hill. A sweet tang of orange, mixed with the soft scent of packed earth, filled the room.

In one corner, an old brick construction with an iron door in the center stood—some sort of fireplace.

Costa moved toward it, his eyes growing wider, a warm smile lighting his face. "I haven't seen one of these for *years*," he said, his hand on the brick top. His voice was suddenly lighter, excited even. "In the old days you'd have to light a fire in here to get hot water." He touched an old faucet that sat over the bath. "My grandparents had one. They used the hot water for washing clothes...or themselves."

Summer shuddered. She could just imagine her mother here in the eighties, with goodness knows how many other hippies, incense burning, wallowing about all day in the bath, and singing about peace, love and understanding.

Her dream bathroom floated through her imagination—all white tiles and halogen lights, big fluffy towels and a healthy looking fern in the corner.

Costa turned to face her and leaned back against the fireplace as a mysterious look flitted across his face. "What if I was to say there *is* a way around this, a way for you to legally renovate and sell before you leave the country?"

Blood rushed to her core and Summer gave up a silent vote of thanks for whomever had sent her this wonderful man. "I'd say I'll do whatever it takes," she said, unable to stop the smile that began to push its way across her face. "Tell me—"

He held up a hand. "First I need to know how long you've got."

For a moment she wanted to fall into his soul-searching eyes. Shaking her head she took a step back. "What do you mean?"

"How long do you intend to stay?"

"Four weeks. That's all the time I've managed to take from work. I'd imagined I could sell this place quite quickly, in which case I could've gone home sooner..."

A sudden scuffle in the ceiling directly above made her leap back and she let out a small squeal at the thought something might fall on her.

"Looks as though *someone* likes living here," Costa said as they both looked up.

When he glanced back at her, his eyes softening, she

could finally see a funny side to all this and for the first time she felt the warmth of his concern.

"I'll tell you what I'll do," he said. "I'm back in the village for about four weeks too. If you agree with my plan, I think we could get this finished in a month. I can't guarantee you're going to like my idea though."

"Even if there is a way for me to renovate legally, I don't have the *money* to do it," Summer said in desperation. Was he offering to pay for the work himself? Surely not. She'd never be beholden to someone like that.

"I can help you sort out a builder, a plasterer, and," he said, thumping the tap again, "maybe a plumber. It shouldn't take too long to make this place habitable."

She was grateful, of course she was, but it still didn't solve her two major problems: finding a way around the law and, if she managed *that*, finding money for the renovations. The thought that working every day with Costa could also be a very big problem was almost enough to make her turn and run right now.

"So you can pay for it," Costa said as he watched the light shine behind her eyes, "I'm sure I can help you find a job or two around the village."

As he spoke, Costa made a conscious effort to hide the panic plowing through him. He'd made a promise to ensure Summer left the island with everything she'd come for, and he sure as hell wasn't going to renege on it. But he hadn't counted on *this* set of circumstances.

And he'd promised she'd never find out who'd really sent him here.

She wasn't what he'd expected. Stunning, yes, but he had to ignore that fact and the stirring it caused in him right from the outset. He had a task to complete in as short a time as possible and, given the restrictions they were both under, the only solution to their problem was beginning to flash neon in his head.

Although her mother had written of a materialistic girl without spirit, Costa could see parts of her mother in her. Cropped blonde hair stood in stroppy little spikes, whereas her mother's hair had been long and loose. Even though he was only a boy then, he could remember the same delicate features he saw now.

Summer wore shorts, revealing perfect legs. Quite a contrast to his hippy teacher with her flowing skirts. But it was the pendant that lay on the pale skin of her throat that reminded him of something Summer's mother might have treasured.

Although they'd been corresponding by letter throughout the course of her illness, it had been years since he'd seen Caroline. He remembered the day when, as a boy, his whole class and most of the village had gone down to the jetty to wave her goodbye, everyone in tears. He'd never forgotten her, had always remembered what she'd taught him, and what he *owed* her. He remembered a vibrant, carefree person, certainly not someone as uptight as the woman who stood in front of him now.

He didn't like secrets, but when Caroline had written and explained she didn't have long to live, he'd promised her anything—he'd always be in her debt and was prepared to do whatever she asked. Knowing her daughter would have to travel to Greece to claim the house, Caroline had asked if he'd look out for her only child, insisting Summer mustn't know about their communication and that he mustn't help her out financially. Apparently, her daughter was frighteningly independent.

He hoped it wouldn't take long, that he could leave this

place —this town that seemed to close in on him—and get back to where he belonged as quickly as possible. It was vital that his time here be kept a secret, away from the prying lenses and crude questions the paparazzi would often fire at him. The villagers would hate it if the gossip-hungry hordes overran the town the way they did the last time he was here. He'd had to take a detour coming to the island yesterday when one particularly rabid journalist popped up in Athens airport.

It was stupid of him to overlook the renovation rule. There was one simple way around that though—but he couldn't imagine she'd agree to it.

"What sort of job could I do here to raise the money?" Summer said, her small brow furrowing deeper. "I don't have a work permit to earn cash, but what if I could make something, do something in exchange?" Her eyes grew wider.

Not for the first time that day, Costa thought how unnecessarily difficult this was going to be. Caroline had insisted he mustn't give Summer money, but it would be so much easier if he did. Her body language—the folded arms, the permanent little frown—made it clear she didn't want to be here either.

"You could teach English," he said, picking up on her idea. "Lots of people have learned English at school, but they're always looking to improve. I'm sure you could trade an hour or two for some plumbing, a conversation or two for some building. Maybe even help out at the school."

Her head tilted a little to the side and he could feel her indecision as she stuttered, "Oh, I don't think I'd be...I wouldn't know how to begin *teaching* someone."

Why was she so flustered? Her mother had been an inspirational teacher.

"I think you could," he said, fascinated by the way he could almost see the cogs working behind her luminous blue eyes. She wanted an easy way out of this, but it wasn't going to happen. What they'd have to do was the last thing he'd choose, but he would never go back on a promise.

"Do you think so?" For a second, calm seemed to cross her face and for the first time her gaze truly met his. Hope radiated out of their blue depths and something pulled tight in his chest.

Another scuffle in the roof.

Costa watched as her eyes moved to the ceiling in obvious apprehension, the milky skin of her neck stretching.

Her face was pale and without makeup. A blonde fringe fell across her forehead, making her appear younger than he guessed she was. Her lips, pressed together right now, held promises he imagined stealing if the moment were right...

When her gaze turned back to him, her teeth were gritted and she let out a sigh as she pulled the small pink bead from her pocket. "So tell me, how do we get around this rule? I'm prepared to do whatever it takes to get this place saleable. What do I have to do to get started?"

Costa looked down at her, his pulse beginning to harden as the words fell from his mouth before he'd truly thought them through. It was crazy and it was outrageous, but it was what he had to do to honor the memory of her mother.

"There's only one way," he said, as he watched her eyes widen. "All you have to do is marry me."

Buy *A Home for Summer* from your local book store, amazon.com, or ask for it at your local library.

Multi award winning author, Barbara DeLeo's first book, co-written with her best friend, was a story about beauty queens in space. She was eleven, and the sole, handwritten copy was lost years ago much to everyone's relief. It's some small miracle that she kept the faith and now lives her dream of writing sparkling contemporary romance with unforgettable characters.

Degrees in English and Psychology, and a career as an English teacher, fueled Barbara's passion for people and stories, and a number of years living in Europe —primarily in Athens, Greece—gave her a love for romantic settings.

Discovering she was having her second set of twins in two years, Barbara knew she must be paying penance for being disorganized in a previous life and now uses every spare second to create her stories.With every word she writes, Barbara is sharing her belief in the transformational power of loving relationships.

Married to her winemaker hero for twenty two years, Barbara's happiest when she's getting to know her latest cast of characters. She still loves telling stories about finding love in all the wrong places, but now without a beauty queen or spaceship in sight.

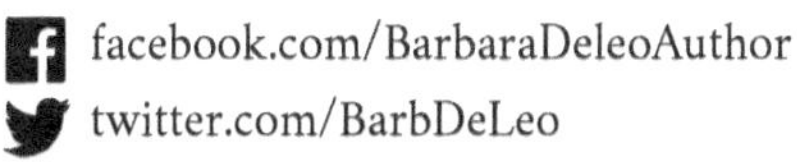

**If you really enjoyed *Reining in the Rebel* and fancy reading a lot more about the crazy, lovable Katsalos family, as well as Barbara's next series, apply to join Barbara's review team!**

Barbara is now taking applications to join her Advanced Review team. If you're selected, you'll get all of Barbara's releases free, up to a month before release!

Email barb@barbaradeleo.com and Barbara will be in touch!

# ACKNOWLEDGEMENTS

Not only was I lucky enough to have been born into a wonderfully supportive family where dreams are championed and crazy little quirks celebrated, I've been welcomed into a second family too. Since I met my Greek boyfriend, now husband, thirty years ago, I've been immersed in a culture, a language, and a way of celebrating life that I love. I'd like to thank both families for giving me love, laughter, and inspiration for the story of the Katsalos family in my *Tall, Dark and Driven* series.

My heartfelt thanks also goes to:

My agent, Nalini Akolekar, who always has my back and wonderful advice to share.

My incredible crit partners, Hayson Manning and Rachel Bailey, who are amazing writers and save my patootie time and time again.

Iona, Sue, Kate, Courtney, Deborah and Nadine who are the BEST group of motivators, cheerleaders and wine drinking pals a girl could have.

My cover designer, Natasha Snow, who nails it every time.

My copy editor Elizabeth King whose Type A attention to detail is legendary.

And to George and my four amazing children, thank you for helping me to keep on living this dream. Squeeze, squeeze, squeeze.

***Barb*** X

www.ingramcontent.com/pod-product-compliance
Lightning Source LLC
Chambersburg PA
CBHW030739110726
47900CB00008B/2366